28-2-92

The Poisoned Web

Patience Merriman was old, frail and frustrated. She had once reigned over an Oxford salon in the days when her professor husband was alive. Now the love of power and talent for intrigue which had made her a force in Oxford society were expended on her own household: on the two young students occupying the top floor whose relationship she aimed to destroy; on her only child, whom she had never forgiven for being a daughter, and who she alleged was seeking her death.

Romola Merriman certainly had every provocation to matricide, but was the old woman telling the truth, or was it one more of the malicious rumours she loved to circulate – a rumour which might this time come true? For Patience did not care if she caused a death, directly or indirectly, and others were soon tempted to cause hers – to save themselves or to save Romola. Who would win in this battle of wits and wills?

ANNA CLARKE

The Poisoned Web

THE CRIME CLUB

COLLINS, ST JAMES'S PLACE, LONDON

William Collins Sons & Co Ltd
London · Glasgow · Sydney · Auckland
Toronto · Johannesburg

First published 1979
© Anna Clarke, 1979
ISBN 0 00 231647 1
Set in Baskerville
Made and Printed in Great Britain by
William Collins Sons & Co Ltd Glasgow

CHAPTER I

'July 31, 1978,' wrote Mrs Patience Merriman in her large round handwriting at the top of the first page of the new red exercise book. 'I am so frightened. I am sure Romola is planning to murder me.'

She paused a moment when she heard the click of the garden gate and glanced up through the window by which she sat all day and through which she had an excellent view not only of the front garden of Beechcroft but also of the greater part of St Helen's Road. It was a short cul-de-sac leading off the Woodstock Road in Oxford, and Beechcroft was a large semi-detached house built in red brick at about the turn of the century.

Mrs Merriman was eighty-four and arthritis had very nearly deprived her of the use of her legs. But her eyesight was still good and her hearing was particularly acute, while her mind was no less clear than it had been fifty years ago when as the wife of an eminent Oxford historian she had been a sparkling and witty hostess whose invitations were much sought after.

'One of the young folk from the top flat going out,' she wrote in the notebook. 'I think it was the boy, Laurie, but it's so difficult to tell nowadays because they all look exactly alike, particularly from the back.'

Again she paused, letting her pen drop on to the table and leaning back in her chair. The arthritis in her hands was nothing like as bad as that in her legs, but it was still a great effort to write for more than a few minutes at a time. Besides, she wanted to think. The whole point of writing what she was writing now was that it should come to the eyes of one or other of the students who rented the attic flat and it would therefore not be very sensible to make tactless comments about the youth of today.

Mrs Merriman rested her hands together, the right clasped over the left, in her lap. It didn't really still the pain, and yet in some obscure way the hands comforted each other. There was power in them still, and there was also power in her eyes and her ears and above all in her mind and in her will. Aged and crippled she might be, but the power within her was capable of controlling and manipulating abler bodies than her own, and so she was not so helpless after all, whatever Romola might think.

Romola had gone into Oxford to have her hair done. As if that would make her look any better. At forty-eight she was an angular, awkward woman, just as at eight she had been a clumsy and nervous little girl. Whatever had Professor Francis Merriman and his brilliant and beautiful wife Patience done to deserve no issue but this? They ought to have had three sons, one a scholar, one an artist, and one rather wild and troublesome but none the less the darling of their hearts.

Instead of which there was nothing but Romola, a girl without beauty or character.

'I was afraid it might be Romola coming back,' wrote Mrs Merriman now that her hands were a little rested. 'I know she is plotting something against me. She wants to be rid of me to have this house to herself. But whether she is hoping to get me put into a nursing home or whether she is actually planning to murder me . . .'

Mrs Merriman put down her pen for the last time. That would be enough. No need to write any more. Anyone chancing to read that entry or even nothing but the first sentence of it would immediately get the message. But how to get it into their hands, that was the question. For a moment she considered the possibility of dropping it out of the window on to the bed of petunias beneath. The red exercise book would show up clearly even among the bright flowers, and somebody would be bound to notice it and bring it into the house.

The trouble was that that somebody might be Romola, and although it would not necessarily be fatal to Mrs Merriman's plan if her daughter were to read what she had just written, on the whole she would rather Romola did not see it. But if it was one or both of the young people who found the diary, there was still no guarantee that they would read it. That was the trouble with so many young people nowadays, thought Patience Merriman impatiently: not that they were the selfish promiscuous layabouts of the popular cartoons, but that they were so painfully serious about the troubles of the world and so absurdly reluctant to indulge in little dishonesties and deceptions. It came from being too free and having too much come to them too easily. They didn't have to plot and scheme and study other people and play the hypocrite to get what they wanted, and so they could indulge themselves with the luxury of a tender conscience about such matters as reading other people's private papers.

No, she could by no means rely on either Laurie Kingston or Brenda Long to read the words that she had just written deliberately for them to read. And in any case, if she threw the exercise book out of the window it would get soaking wet and the ink would run. The rain was still coming down relentlessly, as it had been doing ever since breakfast-time. And it was getting cold too.

Mrs Merriman stretched out her right hand and pulled the casement window shut.

The action brought her comfort. At least there were a few things that she could still do for herself. Like manipulating her chair at great speed across the room, which she now proceeded to do, opening the door with its handle specially designed for cripples like herself, and wriggling the chair out into the front hall. If she liked she could roll across to the room opposite, which was now fitted up as her bedroom, or even further along to the downstairs washroom and lavatory where she could still, thank heaven, manage for herself. When that last indignity came and she was no longer able to do so, then would be the moment to loose her grip on life, but meanwhile the long and painful and restless nights were still tolerable because there was plenty to interest her in the days that followed them and she most certainly did not want to die just yet.

The front hall of Beechcroft was large and square but at the moment rather dark, because the only natural light came from two slits of windows either side of the big front door. Their small diamond-shaped panes were of a yellowish tint, and on this dull wet summer afternoon the hall had all the sinister mystery of a November fog. There were electric light switches just inside the front door and at the foot of the stairs, but Mrs Merriman made no movement towards them. Now that she had decided what to do she was quite content to wait patiently in the gloomy hall until somebody came in. Then she would act according to who that somebody was. There was no need for her to see them before she acted. She would know which one of them it was from the sound of the footsteps on the gravel drive and in the porch. Even the click of the gate sounded differently when Romola shut it from how it did when one of the young people shut it, and in any case if it were Romola she would hear the car. She would also know at once if it were none of the three other people living in the house, but a visitor or someone begging or trying to sell something at the door.

The only thing she could never be quite sure about until she saw them full face was which one of the two young people it was, the boy or the girl. They were so very alike in their shabby blue jeans and skimpy tops, much the same height and both with short springy dark hair that Mrs Merriman rather admired. She was glad that the long straggly rats' tails had for the most part gone out of fashion again among the young. But she might be able to tell which one of them it was on this occasion because Brenda's footstep was the lighter, in spite of the clumpy-soled shoes that she wore.

On the whole Mrs Merriman hoped that it would be Laurie who came in first. She was quite sure that women were more inquisitive and therefore more likely to read other people's papers, even serious-minded students of literature like Brenda Long, but her own personal preference was always for men. She did not like women at all and was never quite at ease with them. But men were all the same at bottom and did not change much from one generation to another. Laurence Kingston, young history scholar just about to embark on his doctorate, was much the same under the skin as Professor Francis Merriman at the height of his powers and his fame. All of them had the same sort of weaknesses that made them so easy to manipulate if only you knew how. And Mrs

Merriman had no doubt at all that she knew exactly
how to manipulate anybody.

She closed her eyes and relaxed in her chair, waiting
and listening, with the red exercise book folded open at
the first page lying in her lap.

CHAPTER II

'HI! BRENDA!'

Laurie ran round the corner of St Helen's Road to try
to catch up Brenda, who was cycling quickly along with
her head down against the still driving rain. He reached
out and got hold of the back mudguard, causing Brenda
to put a foot down on the kerb and look round indignantly.

'What on earth . . .' She had not heard him call.
'Hullo, darling,' she said with a change of expression
when she saw him and they gave each other a quick little
hug, there on the pavement in the rain, with the bicycle
propped up by its saddle against Brenda's wet thigh.

'No work for you this afternoon?' she said as they
walked on together, with Laurie pushing the bike and
Brenda's arm round his waist.

'No luck,' he replied. 'Well, would you want to go on a
guided tour round Oxford in this weather?'

'Not really, but I'd have thought some of the Americans
would be keen enough. They've spent all that money
getting here. They might as well see the place.'

'Oh, they're not wasting their time,' replied Laurie.
'They've all gone off in coachloads to see Blenheim Palace.
That keeps them out of the rain for a good three hours.
They offered me a party to take round if I liked, but

somehow the prospect of a whole afternoon of bored and gawping faces . . .' His voice tailed away and a moment later he added apologetically: 'I'm sorry, Bren. I know we need the money. I'm lucky to get this sort of vacation job and not be stuck on a conveyor belt. I won't play hookey again, I promise. I'll take anything they give me even if it means climbing St Mary's spire with two dozen camera-clicking Japanese.'

He shifted the bicycle to his right hand, put the other one round the girl's shoulders, and smiled at her. He had an angular clean-shaven face and a mouth that smiled readily. He was a very conscientious and hardworking boy, but every now and then he would say or do something rather unexpected that never failed to surprise Brenda, who was a conventional soul at heart and never subject to such aberrations herself. She loved him very dearly, though, and this gave her the wisdom not to reproach him for losing them the whole afternoon's pay that they needed to keep up the modest home that meant so much to them.

For they were both children of broken homes, these two young people who appeared to be so free and so privileged, with the whole world before them. Both of them had that dull jagged-edged pain at heart that comes from torn loyalties; it was this that had drawn them together in the first place and would keep them together for life. No amount of formal vows and legal ceremonies could possibly forge a stronger link between them than their mutual need to repair that jagged edge and build themselves a home, although they fully intended to get married once their lives were more settled and either one or the other of them was earning a regular salary.

'Never mind,' said Brenda, who was working mornings and evenings at a snack bar while applying for the few more suitable jobs that were available in this era of high unemployment. 'We'll have my week's wages and we're terribly lucky to be paying such a low rent for such a gorgeous flat. Aren't we, darling?' she added as Laurie did not immediately respond.

'Yep. Very low rent. Very lucky,' he replied. 'Wish I knew why, that's all.'

'Oh, Laurie.' Brenda was reproachful. They crossed the road and came to the double iron gates that served both the drive to the garage and the path to the front door of Beechcroft. One of the gates was hanging open, leaving room to push the bicycle through. 'Mrs Merriman's explained why the flat is so cheap,' said Brenda as they walked along to the little garden shed where they kept their bicycles because there was not room in the garage for them alongside Romola's big Austin. 'She doesn't need the money and she's only taking tenants because she feels she ought to do something for the university. And because she likes young people and doesn't even mind them not being married, which I think is wonderful of her considering her age.'

'Yes, that's what she said,' agreed Laurie.

He pulled open the door of the shed, straightened the bicycle and positioned it carefully, then let go of the handlebars and gave it a vigorous push from behind the saddle. It shot straight forward into the gap between the lawn-mower on one side and his own bike, at present paralysed by a puncture, on the other side, and came to rest neatly against the latter.

'Good shot, Kingston!' cried Laurie in infantile triumph. 'Right first time.'

As he shut the door of the shed he rather wished, as he did from time to time, that it was Brenda who had made this remark and not himself. There was no question at all about his feeling for her, but he did occasionally wish that she did not always act as if she had the burden of the whole world on her shoulders. As it was, he sometimes appeared as if he were much more clownish and frivolous than he really was because he had to provide all the light-heartedness for the two of them.

But this time he did have a pleasant little surprise. Brenda actually smiled quite merrily. 'You're a big baby and I love you,' she said. 'And if you keep bowling wickets with my bike like that you'll give it a puncture too. When are you going to mend your own?'

'Now. Might as well. D'you think Miss Merriman would mind if I do it in the garage? Or is she likely to come back any minute? Funny sort of day for her to be taking the old girl for a drive. They can't have gone far.'

He was already in the garage, fixing up to mend the puncture, as he was speaking. Brenda watched him for a moment or two in silence.

'Anything I can do?'

'No, thanks. Why don't you go and put the kettle on? It's more or less tea-time. At any rate I feel like it. I won't be long.'

Brenda looked at her watch. She had a tendency to stick to regular set times for meals that not even three years as a student at Oxford had entirely eliminated. 'It's twenty past three,' she said. 'I think I'll put some dry clothes on first. I'm soaked through.'

'So am I. But I might as well finish the dirty work before I have a bath. Don't take all the hot water.' He looked up at her from where he was kneeling on the garage floor and she bent over and their lips met briefly.

'Bye for now,' said Brenda and ran back along the drive to where it branched off into the gravel path that led to the front door.

So it was Brenda, after all, who was the first to come into the house. Mrs Merriman, who had heard them come in at the gate and had made a little sally into her bedroom which had a window at the garage side of the house, had actually overheard quite a lot of their conversation and was not feeling too pleased with Laurie in consequence.

When Brenda pushed open the front door the hall light suddenly came on, which was rather disconcerting to the girl because she had thought there was nobody in the house. She blinked and became aware of Mrs Merriman's chair stationed between the bottom of the stairs and the door of the big sitting-room. Brenda, still startled, knew instantly that there was something about Mrs Merriman's position that worried her, but it was not until later on that she realized what that something was. At the time she simply said feebly: 'Hullo, Mrs Merriman. I didn't know you were there. I thought you'd gone out for a drive.'

'No, my dear. Not on such a miserably wet day.'

Mrs Merriman began to shift her chair towards the open door of the sitting-room, making rather a clumsy job of it. Brenda hastened forward to help her.

'Where do you want to be?' she asked.

'My usual place. By the window. Thank you so much, Brenda. What a kind girl you are.'

The delicate little face, still pink-complexioned and crowned with a mass of soft and pure white hair, tilted up against the back of the chair. Brenda looked down at the old lady and marvelled afresh, as she did every time she saw her, that anybody could still look so extraordinarily pretty when they were crippled and over eighty, and in particular, that anybody in constant pain and leading such a dreary life could have such a sweet smile.

Mrs Merriman really was a most wonderful old lady, and Brenda could not understand why Laurie was always a bit funny about her and inclined to be sorry for Romola. For if she, Brenda, had had a mother like Mrs Merriman instead of a slovenly, complaining, never-satisfied mother who had driven Brenda's own father away and now flitted about from one unsatisfactory substitute to another, Brenda would not have minded how much she did for her. She would have admired and loved her and devoted herself to her as she had never felt able to devote herself to her own mother, much to her own shame and guilt.

'Can I do anything for you, Mrs Merriman?' she asked. 'Shall I bring you some tea? I was just going to make some.'

'That's very sweet of you,' was the reply, 'but I think perhaps I had better wait until my daughter gets back. She might be offended if you made it and I wouldn't want to upset her. In fact I dare not upset her.'

The charming little face looked up at Brenda again, but this time there was something wistful in the smile and also something else. The old lady looked really nervous. More than nervous: really quite frightened. Brenda found herself becoming indignant towards the absent Romola Merriman and a new idea shot into her head that she decided to mention to Laurie the moment they were alone. Mrs Merriman was afraid of her odd and moody daughter. She was completely dependent on her but she didn't like being alone in the house with her, and that was why she took in student-tenants at such a low rent and treated them so generously, really making them feel as if this was their own home. It was because she felt they were a protection for her against her daughter.

That made good sense and explained the mystery, if there were indeed a mystery. Surely Laurie would be able to see that.

Brenda smiled back at the old lady reassuringly. She would have liked to say, 'Don't worry, Mrs Merriman. You've got us here to keep an eye on you,' but decided that it might be better if she didn't. It might be presuming too much, for after all she and Laurie had only been living at Beechcroft for a few weeks and it was not as if they knew the Merrimans really well. So instead she simply said: 'Are you sure there's nothing else that I can do for you?'

'I don't think so, thank you, my dear.'

Mrs Merriman stretched out a hand to open the casement again. Brenda instantly forestalled her, and as she was a tall girl and her head was a long way above that of the little old woman cradled in her big movable chair, Brenda did not see the expression of viciousness and frustration on Mrs Merriman's face as the little task of opening the window was taken away from her. By the time Brenda had moved back again the sweet smile was once more in place.

'There is just one thing you could do if you would be so kind,' said Mrs Merriman. 'I have stupidly left my note-book on the dressing-table in the bedroom. It's the one I use as a diary. Not that there is anything much to record, but it whiles away the hours. I scribble all sorts of non-sense in it. Do you keep a diary, Brenda?'

Brenda replied that she had once done so, at a very

unhappy time of her life, when her parents' marriage was in process of coming apart.

'It helped to write it down,' she added. 'I didn't want to tell any of my friends about it. It didn't seem fair to Dad.'

Mrs Merriman made suitably sympathetic noises. 'You know you have always got a home here, Brenda,' she said earnestly. 'Or at least for as long as I have any say in the matter. I love to have you both about the place. But of course I am so very helpless. I only hope that nothing . . .'

Her voice faded away. Her face took on again that shrinking and fearful expression.

'You will find the notebook on my dressing-table, I believe,' she said briskly a moment later. 'It's a red exercise book. You can't mistake it. Thank you again.'

Brenda left the room and Mrs Merriman stared after her retreating figure with hatred in her eyes. Her lips quivered and for a few seconds continued to make the involuntary chewing movements of old age. She raised her left hand and pressed her fingers to her mouth to steady it. Then she reached out with her right hand, took hold of the catch of the casement window, and pulled it shut again with a savage little click. After that she lay back in her chair as if the effort had exhausted her, and waited with closed eyes for the girl to return with the red exercise book.

CHAPTER III

'But I couldn't have seen it more clearly!' exclaimed Brenda. 'I'm not imagining it, Laurie. Honestly. I don't imagine things, do I?'

'No, love. You don't imagine things,' agreed Laurie. Indeed, for a student of literature Brenda was singularly lacking in imagination. She was conscientious and thorough and was good at weighing up different points of view and summarizing them, and it was these qualities that had gained her at any rate a respectable degree. Her ambition was to be a reporter or a theatre critic, but Laurie secretly thought that Brenda would have made an excellent nurse. She was never so happy as when she was looking after somebody, and sometimes Laurie thought she was a little disappointed in his own excellent health. He did not think she had any hope at all of fulfilling her ambitions, not in a tough and competitive field where her rivals would be much better at selling themselves than she could ever be. But it would be kindest, he thought, to let her find this out gradually for herself, and in any case it didn't matter much what Brenda did because he, Laurie Kingston, was certainly destined to go straight to the top in the academic world and he would eventually be making enough money for them both.

Meanwhile they had a problem on hand. At least Brenda thought of it as a problem. If Laurie had happened to read the entry in Mrs Merriman's diary, he believed that he would simply have ignored it; or at any rate he would have put a different interpretation on it and he probably would not have mentioned it to Brenda at all.

'I'm quite sure it said what you say it did,' he continued, helping himself to another piece of toast.

The tea-tray lay between them on the hearthrug. Laurie had switched on the light of the coal-effect electric fire, not because it was cold but because it was such a dismal day and he felt they could both do with a little cheering up. Brenda had made no protest at this minor extravagance.

'It said, "I'm so frightened because I'm sure my daughter is planning to murder me",' repeated Brenda. 'I know I ought not to've read it but I couldn't really help it. There were two red notebooks lying there and I had to open them to see which one it was she wanted, and when I opened this one it just jumped out at me.'

'Yes, love, I can see that,' said Laurie. He wondered whether to suggest that it might have been intended to jump out at her in this manner, but decided not to put forward this theory just yet. It was never wise to start speculating until you had collected all your facts together, or at any rate as many facts as were available to you, and the main thing at the moment was to calm Brenda down, because she was very distressed, both at having read somebody else's private document, an act which she greatly disapproved of, and also at what she had seen in that document.

It would not comfort her at all to believe she had been intended to read it; it would only make her feel more responsible than ever for the safety of Mrs Merriman, and Laurie saw it as his task at the moment to try to stop Brenda feeling so responsible for their landlady.

'I wish I didn't have to go to the snack bar this evening,' she said. 'I wish I could stay here and keep an eye on her.'

'I'll keep an eye on her if it's necessary,' said Laurie. 'I'm not going out.'

Brenda did not look as relieved as he had hoped she would. She glanced round the pleasant little sitting-room that had been made out of one of the top-floor bedrooms at Beechcroft and then lowered her voice as if not convinced that they were not being overheard.

'There's another thing. I'm sure Romola was in the house when I came in but disappeared before I could see her.'

'What had she done with the car, then?'

'I don't know. Taken it in for servicing, perhaps. But I'm sure she was there lurking somewhere.'

'Lurking!' Laurie did not entirely keep the note of mockery out of his voice. 'What a word to use. For heaven's sake, Brenda, it's the woman's own house. She's a perfect right to lurk in it if she wants to.'

'It isn't her house. It's Mrs Merriman's.'

'How d'you know?'

'She told me.'

'When?'

'Last Saturday afternoon. When Romola had gone shopping and I helped Mrs Merriman get her chair down to the lawn. I do think it was mean of Romola not to get her mother out into the sun, considering it was about the only fine day we've had this summer.'

Laurie made no comment on this. 'Why did you think Romola was in the house when you came in this afternoon?' he asked.

'Because the light in the hall came on just as I opened the front door. It gave me quite a fright. And it couldn't have been Mrs Merriman turning it on because she wasn't close enough to either of the switches. So it must have been Romola switching it on from the first-floor landing.'

'So what? Even if it isn't her house it's her home. She's every right to turn the lights on and off as she likes.'

'Then if she was in, why wasn't she downstairs helping her mother to get back into the sitting-room after going to the loo?'

'Why the hell should she be?' exclaimed Laurie, with the exasperation now showing only too plainly in his voice. 'The poor woman doesn't have to be fussing over her mother every second of the day. She has scarcely any life of her own as it is. And if she's to be grudged every half hour that she does manage to snatch to do what she wants to do . . .'

'Mrs Merriman can't help being crippled with arthritis,' said Brenda stiffly.

'Nobody's suggesting she can. Of course she needs looking after. But it wouldn't surprise me at all if what she can do and what she can't do varies a great deal from day to day and from hour to hour.'

'I expect it does,' said Brenda. 'That's the nature of the disease.'

'I didn't mean that,' said Laurie, goaded by her coolness into saying what he had not intended to say. 'I mean she varies her condition according to her audience. Pulls out all the stops and gets all the sympathy when she's with some people and puts on a brave show of coping with infirmity when she's with others. It wouldn't surprise me at all to find she could manage lots of things when she's alone that even Romola doesn't know she can do. She probably turned that light on herself and then whizzed the chair round so quickly that you didn't know she'd moved. Or she could have pushed down the switch with the end of her stick. She's got surprisingly good eyesight and a good aim, considering her condition. I've noticed that.'

He stopped suddenly, cursing himself for having been carried away like this, and looked up to see Brenda staring at him with something like hostility.

'I think it's absolutely disgusting to talk about a crippled old woman in that way,' she said. 'Haven't you got any feeling at all?'

Laurie stared at her unhappily before dropping down on to his knees on the hearthrug and wriggling himself across to the chair in which she was sitting. Then he squatted back, put his hands on his knees, looked at her very seriously, and said: 'We're quarrelling, Bren. And we mustn't quarrel. We don't enjoy it. Not like some couples. Let's stop, shall we? Let's try and forget the Merrimans for a little while.'

And he raised both hands and held them out to her. She continued to sit stiff and upright in her chair for the best part of a minute before she relented and slid down on to the hearthrug beside him.

Two floors down, in the big drawing-room with the window that had such a commanding view, Mrs Merriman looked up from her game of patience as her daughter Romola came into the room.

'The boy's a bit oafish, I think,' she said with a contemptuous little twist of the lips.

'What boy are you talking about?'

Romola Merriman had a low and exceptionally pleasant voice. It always surprised people when they first heard it.

Mrs Merriman raised her eyes to the ceiling to indicate who she meant.

'Upstairs? You mean Laurence Kingston?' said Romola.

'Who else? I was not aware that we had changed tenants since this morning.'

'What has he been doing?' Romola sat down in one of the armchairs near the fireplace at the far end of the room and picked up a book. She had cleared away the tea-things and would not be preparing the evening meal for another hour. In winter this was always the worst time of the day, when the curtains were drawn and they were shut in with each other. Summer evenings were not so bad, because this was the hour for watering the garden. But it needed no watering today and it was so dark and dismal that it felt like winter. She opened the book at the page where the marker rested. It was a detective story and presumably she had read those fifty-four pages because she had put the book mark in herself. But she could not remember anything about them, not even who the different characters were. She often felt like this nowadays: completely blank, as if there were no past and no future, unaware of anything except the immediate job to be done or of the task just completed. Even the two hours at the hairdresser's, a blessed little interval of peace once a fortnight, had slipped away from her completely. Would her mother stay playing patience quietly until they switched on the television for the early evening news? That was all there was in Romola Merriman's mind at this moment.

Mrs Merriman saw that Romola was in a state of mental blankness and determined to do something about it. She shuffled the cards together, although she had in fact only just laid out the patience, twisted her chair round so that she faced her daughter, and enlarged on her theme.

'I am not referring to the accent,' she said, 'although one might have expected that after three years at Oxford he would have learnt to speak in what used to be regarded as an educated voice. But it seems to be considered obligatory nowadays in some circles to talk Yorkshire or Lancashire just to show your good working-class background, so we will give him the benefit of the doubt and assume that he talks like that for choice and not because he knows no better.'

Romola turned a page of her book. She was not reading it and her mother knew perfectly well that she wasn't. But she still sat quite motionless. The relentless drip of the acid voice seemed to be taking longer today than it usually did to have its effect on Romola.

'Nevertheless,' continued Mrs Merriman, 'I think Brenda is much too good for him. I had quite a little chat with her this afternoon and got to know her better than I have done up till now. She is a sympathetic and understanding sort of girl and she deserves a good husband. She is quite pretty and I would guess that she is fairly adaptable, and she is intelligent enough to be able to play down her own brains if necessary. I should like to see her married to a young man with a promising career in front of him, possibly in the diplomatic service, and not to that oafish boy.'

The last words were spoken with great viciousness. Romola dropped her book on the floor and the marker fell out. She picked it up and put it back in the wrong place, and then she began to fidget in her armchair, turning the book round and round in her hands and looking all round the room as if she were a prisoner seeking a way of escape, looking everywhere except at her mother.

This was much more satisfactory. This was the normal reaction. When Mrs Merriman spoke again she was almost purring.

'Really I think it would be quite a kindness to the girl to make her see how very much better she could do for herself.'

'No!'

Romola succeeded in putting so much expression into the little monosyllable that Mrs Merriman wondered, not for the first time, whether there really was some talent in this despised daughter of hers that, given proper encouragement, might one day have borne fruit. There were the makings of a real end-of-second-act cliffhanger in that deep vibrating voice exploding into its one little word, and in the way Romola brought down her left hand heavily on to the cover of the book in her lap and held it there this time, stiff and still, with her whole body rigid and no longer trembling, and with her eyes no longer avoiding her mother's but staring straight at her with an unfathomable expression in their dark depths.

Yes, they were good eyes, thought Mrs Merriman. Her father's eyes. Her one good feature. Properly handled, they could have been the making of her. In fact Romola's father, if left to himself, might well have tried to make the most of those eyes and of any other gift that the girl possessed. But Romola's father had been a very busy and sought-after man, much dependent upon his wife for the comfort and smooth running of his life, and she had seen to it that he did not waste his time and his own great gifts fussing over their unpromising child.

A tragic actress. Yes, she might have been that, thought

Patience Merriman complacently. Either that or a singer. There had been a time, when Romola was in her early teens, when a music teacher had actually suggested to Romola's mother that the girl's voice was worth training. Mrs Merriman had practically forgotten the incident. There had been so many similar. The teacher had not persisted after Mrs Merriman informed her that Romola's father had vetoed the idea. Nobody in the little private school to which Romola had been sent would have dreamed of going against Professor Merriman. And equally, nobody suspected that he had never been consulted at all. In fact it was many years later before Romola herself learnt about it, for the music teacher did not believe in encouraging pupils to go against their parents' wishes, and had spoken to Mrs Merriman without the girl's knowledge.

Patience Merriman's mind dwelt with satisfaction on this little piece of family history. Suppose the girl *had* had the makings of a singer in her? That would be an even better revenge for her own never-ceasing hollow ache of disappointment at the lack of sons. To make sure that this miserable substitute, a daily insult to herself, should lead a sterile and hopeless existence, had always been of some comfort to Mrs Merriman. But to know that within this dim creature was a light and fire that she, Patience, had succeeded in all but extinguishing was an even greater source of satisfaction.

Mrs Merriman looked forward with pleasurable anticipation to the scene that was to follow her daughter's violent ejaculation of the briefest of negatives.

CHAPTER IV

'YOU'RE NOT to do that again,' said Romola in the same tone of barely controlled passion. 'I'm not going to have you turning this young couple against each other as you did the last one.'

'The last one?' Mrs Merriman settled herself comfortably in her chair and assumed an air of innocent surprise. 'Do you mean Peter and Linda?'

'I do mean Peter and Linda. They were perfectly harmless and very attached to each other. You deliberately set them at each other's throats.'

'My dear Romola, you flatter me. That a poor old woman like myself should have such influence. Just imagine!' And she gave a self-conscious little giggle.

Romola said nothing but continued to sit stiffly with her dark eyes blazing, a tragedy queen on the verge of some tremendous dramatic gesture of self-sacrifice or defiance or despair. Mrs Merriman's mouth resumed its cruel little smile.

'That girl Linda was an out-and-out slut,' she said. 'Peter was well rid of her. A charming boy. He would have no difficulty in finding a much more suitable girl. Indeed, I believe he has already found one. Terence told me yesterday evening – you'd gone off to church in a huff so you missed him – that he'd seen Peter on the river in a punt with a delightful-looking blonde girl a few weeks ago before they went down for the long vacation.'

This was a side-swipe, a nice reliable little bit of reinforcement for the main battle. Terence Toogood, TT to his students and everyone else in Oxford who knew him, which comprised a large number of people, was a widower in his fifties, a former student of Professor Francis Merriman's and a friend of the family. He was also Laurie's tutor, which was how Laurie and Brenda had come to be introduced to Mrs Merriman and offered the flat. He was a neat, spare man who looked smaller than he actually was because of his precise controlled gestures, his slight stoop, and the steel-rimmed spectacles that he wore. Though a history scholar, he shared Romola's love of music and was almost as knowledgeable on the subject as she was herself. Sometimes they would have quite an animated discussion, and occasionally would even play a piano duet, Terence taking the bass and usually lagging a little behind Romola.

Mrs Merriman's attitude to these very modest pleasures of her daughter's was a somewhat mixed one. She would have liked to prevent Romola from playing the piano entirely, and she did indeed frequently complain that her nerves would not bear the noise. But Terence knew that Romola enjoyed playing, and Mrs Merriman depended rather heavily on Terence to defend her against allegations that she ill-treated her daughter. After all, appearances had to be kept up. If Romola was allowed to play the piano within limits and to talk music to Terence without any interference from her mother, then Terence could quite truthfully say, when Patience Merriman was talked about in college common rooms or at parties in private houses, that she did after all have her daughter's welfare and happiness at heart.

Mrs Merriman had offended so many people that it was rather convenient to be able to retain at least this one champion. Besides, she had a more subtle way of using

Terence as a weapon against Romola that could be used in private, without Terence's knowledge. By encouraging the friendship, if it could be called that, Mrs Merriman had the satisfaction of seeing her daughter really look forward to Terence's visits to Beechcroft. And from that, of course, it was a very short step to assuming that Romola was in love with the man at the same time as impressing upon her how hopeless a passion this was.

In other words Terence Toogood provided quite unwittingly one of the most splendid instruments of mental torture that Mrs Merriman possessed in her armoury against her daughter. It might well be brought into full operation before the present battle came to an end, but for these preliminary skirmishes it was enough to remind her antagonist of the existence of this weapon.

'And I heard,' said Romola, her beautiful voice sounding harsh with the effort of keeping it under control, 'that Linda had had a bad nervous breakdown and will not be coming back to Oxford next term. It must give you great satisfaction to know you have ruined that girl's career.'

Patience Merriman smirked, then composed her face and said with gentle reproof: 'My dear, how you do exaggerate. It's a bad habit that you ought to have grown out of by now. There is far too much sympathy wasted on these so-called student breakdowns nowadays. If a girl cannot continue with her studies because she has a little upset over a boy-friend, then she should never have been up at Oxford in the first place, in my humble opinion. If you can't stand the heat you should get out of the kitchen. Good gracious me, whatever would your father have said to such nonsense! He would most certainly have thought that any student worth his salt should be able to take a few unhappy love-affairs in his stride.'

'He would not,' said Romola between her teeth. 'That's a filthy lie.'

It was indeed. The late Francis Merriman had been not only a fine scholar but a very humane man, deeply concerned for his students and his younger colleagues. His wife would have remedied this if she could, and did her best to modify his sympathy and generosity whenever it came within her powers. But this still left a wide area of his activities over which she had no control, and he was widely remembered not only with respect but also with genuine affection and gratitude by those whom he had helped over a difficult patch in their careers.

Only with his own daughter had he had no success. He had never been allowed to stay close enough to her to give her all his attention and all his help. And he had died believing that Patience must be right; that Romola really was hopelessly stupid and awkward and incapable of standing on her own feet in any capacity whatever, and that without her mother's constant support and advice the girl would be entirely lost. He loved the child of course, and tried to show it; but to find a way through to Romola's heart and mind and try to sow there some of the superabundant talents of his own was something he had never managed to achieve.

And he had died not realizing why he had not achieved this. There was only one blind spot in that otherwise crystal-clear intellect: and that blind spot concerned his wife. He saw only the most venial of her machinations, mostly those designed to secure his own well-being, and he merely smiled at them. And with regard to Romola, while it sometimes seemed to him that her mother was perhaps over-protective towards the girl and didn't try hard enough to make her independent, that too was very understandable in a mother and it was very difficult to blame Patience for it.

Mrs Merriman had done a first-class job in preventing Professor Merriman from ever getting to know his daughter. She had been less successful in preventing Romola from worshipping her father. Knowledge can be withheld and the experience that leads to knowledge can be denied, but there is no power on earth that can stifle the natural impulses of the human heart when that heart wants to give itself. Even if Romola had not been able to see the evidence of her father's character all around her, even if Francis Merriman had been a nonentity whom Patience had succeeded in presenting to his daughter as an ogre, Romola would still have loved him because she had to love somebody, and from very earliest childhood it had been quite plain that there was no way in which she could love her mother.

Mrs Merriman simply shrugged at Romola's defence of Francis. That was another weapon that could be brought in later if necessary, but up till now Romola seemed to be getting nicely upset without the use of these reliable old standbys. She was gripping the unoffending library book as if she would tear right through all its two hundred pages if she could, and her voice was cracking and her face was getting redder and redder. It would not be long now before the breaking-point came and her whole face would crumple up into a soggy mass, with the great painful tears forcing themselves out of her eyes and her whole body shuddering with its sobbing like some powerful engine deprived of the space in which to move.

She would try to get out of the room, of course, before

that point was reached, but she would not quite make it in time, and Mrs Merriman would be able to see it all before she saw Romola's back in its navy-blue linen dress disappear through the door. Really, thought Mrs Merriman, it was almost too easy. Driving Romola to breaking-point was scarcely enough challenge to her own talents nowadays. Perhaps the other little plot that she had on hand would turn out to be of more interest.

But to her surprise and also to her delight, Romola continued to do battle.

'Anyway, it doesn't matter what Father would have thought,' she went on. 'The fact is that you deliberately worked on Peter so that he broke with Linda. They'd be together now if it had not been for you.'

'And just how am I supposed to have done this?' asked Mrs Merriman.

'You kept rubbing in how untidy she was and – '

'As far as I can remember,' interrupted Mrs Merriman, 'and I am sure you will correct me if my memory is at fault, all I did was to suggest that he might like Mrs Ransome to come up and clean the flat for them now and then after she had finished cleaning down here. Was that so very sinful? I was under the impression that Peter regarded it as a generous offer. And Mrs Ransome was quite willing. And after all – ' the voice became a little plaintive – 'this is my house and I must be allowed some interest in its being kept in good condition, even the part of it that is let to tenants. Linda really was a very dirty girl.'

'Peter never minded it till you pointed it out. They were very happy together.'

'Are you suggesting, my dear,' said Mrs Merriman, suddenly becoming dangerously meek, 'that I should abrogate my interest in the maintenance of my own property for fear of offending the susceptibilities of a common little slut?'

Romola shut her eyes and took several deep breaths. After that her convulsive grip on the book relaxed a little and she looked calmer than she had done for several minutes past. Mrs Merriman began to think that she might, after all, need to bring up some of her reserve artillery.

'I don't think there's much point in talking about Peter and Linda any more,' said Romola surprisingly steadily. 'The damage has been done there. It is Laurie Kingston and Brenda Long who are concerning us now. I do not want a repetition of the story. I intend to prevent further such damage.'

'Dear me,' said Mrs Merriman with her little private giggle. 'How very serious and determined you do sound. Just like your dear father when he knew he was in the wrong. That is the very manner in which he used to talk when he felt it necessary to put on a show of authority and determination because he was just about to give way. Of course I always let him think that he had had the last word and never let him know that I realized he had lost the battle. One has to keep up these little subterfuges with men. They are so very touchy about admitting themselves mistaken. But of course you would not know anything about such matters.'

Romola waited till her mother had finished speaking and then ignored everything she had said.

'It's obviously impossible to find out what you are up to,' she said, 'but you must be plotting something or you would never have mentioned that you thought Laurie was oafish. The only way to save them is to get them both out

of here. I shall give them notice in the morning and tell
them that we need the flat for a resident nurse for you.'

'You will do no such thing!' Mrs Merriman's voice was
shrill. For the very first time in all her long series of
battles with her daughter she had momentarily lost the
upper hand.

'In the morning,' repeated Romola standing up, 'and
we will not let the flat again.'

There was a short silence. Patience Merriman turned
her face to the window because she didn't want Romola
to see that she had scored a point for once. Romola stood
drooping, the library book held slackly in the fingers of her
left hand, temporarily exhausted by the effort of standing
up to her mother.

Then Mrs Merriman rallied. She turned her face
round again and looked up at her daughter with her
sweetest smile. The soft white hair stood out round her
face like a halo.

'I'm afraid it's too late,' she said.

'What do you mean, too late?' Romola had been taken
off guard, as was intended.

'I think you will find it very difficult to persuade
Brenda to leave here. The boy might be willing, but he is
hardly likely to go without her. At any rate not yet,'
added Mrs Merriman ominously.

'What have you done to Brenda?' asked Romola,
coming closer to Mrs Merriman's chair and speaking
threateningly and beginning the violent trembling that
showed she was very near to breaking-point after all.

'She's a nice understanding sort of girl, as I said before,'
said Mrs Merriman. 'She has already been kind enough to
come to my aid on several occasions when you yourself

have not been available. In my opinion she would make a very good nurse, particularly for an elderly invalid, scholar or no scholar though she may be. In fact she has expressed considerable concern about my well-being and is very anxious to be of more assistance to me. If you tell Brenda that we require the upstairs flat for a resident nurse, I have a pretty shrewd suspicion that she will put herself forward for that very role.'

The confidence with which this was said was not lost on Romola. To one with so many years of experience of Mrs Merriman's voice and behaviour it was clear that this was no bluff. In some way or another Brenda Long had already become entangled in the spider's web that Mrs Merriman constantly spun around her, which meant that it was almost certainly too late to rescue her and Laurie.

Romola took several steps towards her mother, gripping the book more tightly in her now upraised left hand. She was left-handed, and the muscles of the bare arm showed taut. Romola was a strong woman, used to heavy domestic work and gardening. She held the library book as if it were a weapon that she was about to use. But when she got within a yard of Mrs Merriman's chair, she suddenly stopped short and let her arm drop.

'You are a vicious evil woman,' she said very quietly, 'even though you are my mother. And you do not deserve to live.'

Mrs Merriman, partly because she felt a genuine spasm of fear, but mostly because she had heard Brenda's step in the hall as the girl went off to her evening job, cried out loudly: 'Don't, Romola! Don't! Leave me alone!'

Romola had not heard Brenda's step, nor did she hear

the faint sound of the latch being turned and the door opened a couple of inches.

'You don't deserve to live,' she repeated in a low voice full of menace before she rushed out of the room.

CHAPTER V

HOW STRANGE, thought Mrs Merriman during the minute that Brenda and Romola were silently and with great embarrassment on both sides encountering each other in the hall; strange how sometimes you imagined something or invented a story as part of a scheme you were devising, and that very invention turned out to have some truth in it after all. When she wrote that diary item stating that she feared Romola was planning to murder her, her only intention had been to start something moving, because practically nothing of interest had happened in the house since the present young couple moved in and she was getting dreadfully bored.

In fact she kept no diary and never had done so, and as soon as the fake entry had served its purpose she had torn the page into small pieces and flushed them down the lavatory. There had been plenty of time to do this after Brenda had gone upstairs and before Romola came back from the hairdresser's. But she had been excited by the success of her plan and this had made her less careful than usual, and she had got her chair jammed in the door of the cloakroom and was having difficulty in freeing herself when Laurie had come in from mending his bike.

He had come straight to her help without being asked, had quickly released the chair, said 'All right now?' and barely waited for her to say she was all right before he grinned and waved at her and sped off up the stairs. It was this behaviour that had caused her to make the remark to Romola that had started off the row. She didn't really think Laurie was oafish. In fact he was an attractive boy, a mixture of the clever son she ought to have had and the wild but charming son she ought to have had, and his very personality rubbed in her own disappointment. Besides, she had sensed a certain coolness in him towards her; or rather not so much coolness as lack of response. It caused her to wonder whether after all Laurie would be easy enough to manipulate.

However, it didn't matter now because things had certainly got moving and had taken a different course entirely. Fate had played one of those extraordinary tricks by taking her invention about Romola planning to murder her and making it actually happen, or rather, appear as if it might happen.

'You don't deserve to live,' Romola had said. Very threateningly. Twice. And the second time Brenda, who had read the diary entry although it had not been openly admitted between them that she had read it, had actually heard Romola's threat.

That had not been planned at all. It was a bit of luck, an unexpected bonus. It made the whole situation very interesting indeed, much more intriguing than anything Mrs Merriman had been able to devise up till now. She felt almost embarrassed with her success, rather as if she had asked for a modest little helping of chicken at a restaurant and had been presented with the entire bird.

Meanwhile Romola and Brenda were standing in the hall staring at each other speechlessly. Brenda stepped back instinctively from the doorway of the sitting-room as Romola rushed out. The light in the hall was on and Brenda could see very clearly the older woman's haggard-looking face with the desperate expression in the dark eyes. A faint twinge of pity came to her, in spite of the words she had just overheard, as she realized something of the extent of Romola Merriman's unhappiness. But it was instantly succeeded by the thought, 'She ought not to speak to her mother like that, no wonder Mrs Merriman is so afraid,' and by the determination to make Laurie see that she was right about them and he was wrong.

'Is Mrs Merriman all right?' she said at last, since Romola seemed incapable either of speaking or of moving away.

'Yes,' was the reply, uttered curtly and almost gruffly. 'Why should you think she isn't?'

'She seemed rather upset this afternoon,' said Brenda. 'I wondered if she wasn't very well.'

'It's kind of you to concern yourself about her,' said Romola, still rather harshly, 'but I do assure you that my mother's health is just as usual and that there is no need for you to worry. She has all the care and medical attention she could possibly need.'

This last speech put Brenda's back up. It was so plainly telling her to mind her own business. It reinforced her own suspicions and made her more determined than ever to keep as close a watch as she could on Mrs Merriman, Laurie or no Laurie. In fact she was extremely reluctant to leave the house now and go to her job for the next three hours. But Laurie had gone and lost them an afternoon's pay – and for the first time Brenda began to feel genuinely resentful towards him about this instead of feeling resigned and forgiving – and so it was essential that she at any rate should go out and earn something.

She watched Romola go upstairs to her bedroom on the first floor and then she pushed open the door of the sitting-room again.

'Is there anything I can do for you, Mrs Merriman?' she asked. 'I'll have to go in a minute, but if you need anything fetching . . .'

Patience Merriman produced her long-suffering smile.

'No, thank you, Brenda dear. I'm all right really. Just a little shocked. I expect you heard. We had a slight difference of opinion, nothing serious, but I'm afraid my daughter does sometimes express herself rather violently. It probably comes from frustration, poor thing. She can't help it. I'll soon be feeling better. You run along now or you'll be late.'

'I wish I didn't have to leave you.'

'So do I, Brenda. And I wish you had a more congenial job. Have you ever thought of taking up nursing? I believe you'd be very good at it.'

'Do you really think so?' Brenda looked pleased.

'I do indeed. You are just the sort of girl that an invalid likes to have around. I'd take you on like a shot if I needed an attendant.'

'Oh, Mrs Merriman, I do so wish . . .'

Brenda's voice tailed away.

'As a matter of fact,' said Patience Merriman, 'that was what our little disagreement was about. My daughter thinks she is perfectly capable of doing all those tiresome chores that are involved in looking after an invalid like myself, but I think it's becoming too much for her. She is not as young as she was, and at her time of life . . . well, that's not something that you will need to worry about for many a year, a bonny young girl like you. I was suggesting that we should get a resident nurse-companion for me to ease the burden on her, but she wouldn't hear of it. Of course we should have to offer her the flat, and the last thing I would want would be to turn you out, my dear, but if it should come to that – '

'Oh, Mrs Merriman!' cried Brenda as the old woman suddenly stopped speaking.

'Why, Brenda!' Mrs Merriman's eyes, still unfaded blue, opened wide and sparkled merrily. 'I do believe you would like the job yourself!'

'If only you'd have me – but I've no experience, you know.'

'That doesn't matter. The main thing is to have the right personality. And you've certainly got that. I would gladly pay you a suitable remuneration in addition to allowing you the flat rent free. But of course I didn't have two people in mind, I'm afraid, when I thought of seeking such help. That makes it a bit difficult. We will have to think this over very carefully. But the job is certainly yours, my dear, and at once, starting tomorrow if you would like to give notice at that café of yours tonight.'

'I'll certainly give notice tonight,' cried Brenda. 'In fact I'm going to be so late that they'll probably give me the sack instead. You can't think how pleased I am! It's terribly difficult to get any sort of job at all nowadays, particularly if you're a graduate. And I'd far rather look after you than stand in that kitchen frying onions. I've never liked fried onions in any case and you just can't imagine what the smell's like unless you've actually been in there. When shall I come and talk to you? Won't it be rather too late when I get back tonight?'

'It will be late,' said Mrs Merriman, 'but I don't sleep very much. One doesn't, you know, at my age, and the night hours seem very long. Just you come and knock at my bedroom door when you come in and we'll have a little private talk then. That'll be fun, won't it?'

And the blue eyes sparkled again, as if at the prospect of a great treat in store.

Brenda cycled off to her evening work with her thoughts in some confusion, wondering now that she was out of Mrs Merriman's persuasive presence whether she had after all done the right thing. She was very concerned indeed about the old lady, and she did have a strong caring instinct in her, and she absolutely hated working at the snack bar and would love to be able to earn money in the comfort of Beechcroft and not have to ride back and forth in the rain and late at night. She had no doubt that Mrs Merriman would pay generously and in fact there was everything to be said for taking this offer of a job.

Except for one thing. Laurie would not like it. That was putting it mildly. Laurie would not only not like it; he would be violently against it. In fact he was going to be very angry with her indeed when she told him, as tell him she must, tonight. And they really would have a quarrel. Their first quarrel. Not like that half-hearted little argument this afternoon that had quickly melted away in each other's arms. This was going to be a very serious and fundamental disagreement indeed and it would test their feeling for each other to the utmost.

Would that feeling stand the test? Brenda wished she could be sure that it would. Five hours ago, when she had met Laurie in the road after coming home from her lunch-time stint, she would have said most emphatically that nothing could ever come between them. But now she was not so sure. It was one thing to be deeply committed to each other for two years when you were both students, and all your attitudes and life styles were running in harmony, but it was another matter when you came to the end of your studies and entered the harsh world of reality.

The trouble was that Laurie had not yet entered that world, while Brenda had. Laurie had got a grant for the next two years while he worked for his Doctor of Philosophy, so he would still be in the sheltered and comparatively irresponsible position of a student, while Brenda simply had to earn her living in one way or another from now on. Not only for herself, but to help Laurie, because his grant was not particularly generous. She was not complaining about this: she even accepted the fact that she would probably have to do the most dreary and menial work for a long time because there were so few openings suitable for her capabilities.

But if she had to do this sort of work, surely she had the right to decide how and where she would do it? Surely not even Laurie, with all his prejudice against old Mrs Merriman, could argue that the kitchen at the Blue Parrot snack bar was a pleasanter place in which to earn one's pennies and pounds than the sitting-room and the downstairs bedroom and bathroom at Beechcroft?

All the time Brenda was cycling along, all the time she was throwing those onions into the pan and slapping beefburgers on to the grill, she found herself arguing with Laurie in her mind. She had never done this before and it worried her and made her unhappy but she couldn't stop doing it.

CHAPTER VI

AT THE VERY MOMENT when Brenda was apologizing to the angry manageress for arriving so late for work on a busy evening, Romola Merriman was walking very slowly and quietly up the stairs that led from the first floor of Beechcroft to the flat on the top floor. She had looked over the rail on the first-floor landing to check that her mother was not in the hall below, although this precaution was scarcely necessary, because the upper staircase was not visible to anybody in the front hall. It was a narrow little flight leading off from the far end of the first-floor landing, very inferior to the wide flight that faced you when you came in at the front door. But then the top floor of the house had been designed for servants only and all four rooms had dormer windows and sloping ceilings. Even after the era of resident domestics had come to an end, Mrs Merriman had been reluctant to make use of these rooms for anybody whom she considered her social equal, but to Romola the attic floor had always been somewhere to escape to, somewhere to hide away in her worst griefs and humiliations.

Since her mother had had to remain downstairs entirely, however, Romola's bedroom above the big drawing-room had become her haven, and it had been no hardship to her to give up the attic floor completely when Mrs Merriman suggested that they should turn it into a self-contained flat and let it to deserving students. Romola had been surprised, because she had not at that time fully understood her mother's motives, but on the whole she had been quite pleased.

'It will be rather nice to have some young life about the house,' she had said to Terence Toogood on one of the rare occasions when her mother had not been present.

'H'm.' Terence had looked and sounded very sceptical. 'Young life. I wonder if your mother knows what she is letting you in for.'

'Oh, but surely there must be some students who are decent and hardworking!' cried Romola. 'You've said so yourself often enough. You're always complaining that people think every student is a drug-taking layabout. Aren't you now?'

'Touché,' said Terence, raising his hands apologetically. 'Yes, I have said so, and I hold to it. The great majority of them are sober and righteous and dreadfully worried about their exam results and careers, poor things. But there is the matter of personal habits and appearance, and their taste in music, my dear Romola, might not always coincide with your own.'

'With yours, you mean,' said Romola with a smile. 'It's not my taste that comes to a full stop with Vaughan Williams.'

'Well, if you do succeed in discovering what they see – or rather what they hear – in the hideous cacophony that I will not dignify by the name of music, I shall be grateful if you will pass on your knowledge to me. But I did not only mean record-players. I was thinking of other matters as well. Perhaps it might best be summed up in that appalling jargon phrase "a permissive life style",' concluded Terence carefully, wondering what sort of fantasies, if any, Romola might have about the sex lives of students. They never spoke of such matters, even when their conversations drifted away from music and into local gossip, but Terence often had the impression that there were hidden depths in Romola Merriman. He greatly enjoyed talking to her and found her an interesting subject for speculation.

She had a voice, of course. Terence had discovered that long ago when his wife had still been alive and Romola had occasionally come to visit them on her own. Once they actually persuaded her to join a choir but after a very short while she had resigned from it and they had never been able to understand why. By nature a very straightforward woman, Romola had been secretive on this occasion, and the nearest Terence had ever got to a reason was by means of a hint dropped by Mrs Merriman that there had been a difference of opinion between Romola and the conductor. Since Romola could be very abrupt at times this was not entirely impossible, but Terence still sometimes wondered about it. She seemed to be content enough with the gentle monotony of her days, but he could not help feeling that, apart from her voice, there was something in her character that might one day burst out and surprise them all. Perhaps she had, even now, some rich and passionate secret life. Perhaps she was actually carrying on an affair with some senior member of the university and successfully keeping it from her mother's eagle eye.

If that were the case, then good luck to her, thought Terence; nevertheless in the matter of student love-affairs and morals he felt obliged to proceed with caution.

'If you mean about the boys and girls living together,' Romola had said in the downright manner in which she always spoke to Terence because she felt happy and at ease with him, 'then as far as I'm concerned I don't mind in the least. They can run a brothel here if they like, so long as they don't make too much noise with it. But I don't know whether my mother . . .'

'Your mother,' repeated Terence thoughtfully. 'One would expect her to disapprove of course, but somehow I don't think she will.'

He was right. Patience Merriman, when sounded out tactfully on the subject, said she did not care in the least whether they let the flat to girls or boys or a mixture of both. In fact the first tenants had been three girls sharing. They came through the university accommodation service and they were not a success. Romola was glad when they told her after two months that they had found somewhere else to live, because they really were very noisy and seemed unable to make any attempt to adjust themselves to the rest of the household. She was also relieved, because it saved her the effort of telling them to go herself. It was not till much later that she suspected her mother had been instrumental in their departure, because Mrs Merriman never said anything about them except that they were a dreary lot and that the whole idea was to offer good accommodation to deserving students, young people of character and promise, in whom she would feel able to take a personal interest.

The nature of that personal interest only became plain to Romola when the second letting came to an end with the total break-up of what had appeared to be a permanent and happy relationship. Romola had watched with helpless distress her mother's manipulation of Peter and Linda. Not only was it horrible in itself, but it brought home to Romola more clearly than ever before the manner in which she herself, her whole life through, had been trapped by her mother like a fly in a spider's web.

It hurt her to see the young folks' bewilderment and

unhappiness. It did more than hurt to look back over her own life with this clearer vision. She tried to prevent the flat being let again, but Mrs Merriman outwitted her by arranging through Terence, who like his teacher Francis Merriman before him was curiously blind to Patience Merriman's darker side, for Laurie and Brenda to have the flat.

With Terence and her mother against her, and only her own deep inner certainty on her own side, Romola was powerless. But as the weeks wore on and the young couple came to no harm she began to feel more comfortable, though still always wary. She took some pains to get to know them, without intruding on their privacy, in the hope of gaining their friendship and counteracting her mother's evil influence, and she felt that she had made some progress with Laurie. That was why she was creeping upstairs now, unsuspected, she hoped, by her mother.

The door at the top of the staircase was standing wide open but nevertheless Romola gave it a little tap.

'Hang on! I'm just coming!' came Laurie's voice, and a moment or two later he appeared, pulling a tee-shirt down over his jeans, his hair damp and generally looking as if he had just got out of a bath.

Romola did not waste time by apologizing for having come up at an inconvenient moment. This neglect of what Mrs Merriman called the social niceties had been the cause of many a lecture from mother to daughter when Romola had been a young girl, but as time wore on Patience Merriman changed tactics and instead of attempting to get her daughter to conform against her will, she made the most of Romola's brusqueness and 'awkwardness' and sometimes gave the impression, to people who did not know them well, that Romola was so gauche as to be practically half-witted. But those few people who really knew and liked Romola, which included one who not only liked but loved her, valued her for this very quality. Most of them were men. On the whole women, whether young or old, did not know what to make of her. She was an adequate cook and housekeeper but seemed to have no interest in talking of domestic matters or of clothes; on the other hand she could not be classed as an intellectual because she had not even got a university degree, let alone any of the other status guidelines by which one could judge people's position in society.

'Can you spare me a few minutes?' said Romola to Laurie.

She had spent some time in her bedroom trying to compose herself after the encounter with her mother, but she still looked rather distraught. Laurie knew nothing of the latest developments downstairs but he guessed that some sort of crisis had been reached.

'I was just about to cheer myself up with the end of a bottle of sherry,' he said. 'It's all we've got in the place. Share it with me?'

'Thanks. I will,' replied Romola.

Laurie fetched two glasses and took great pains to ensure that they should contain equal amounts of sherry. When he had finished pouring, he squatted down beside the table in the little living-room and studied them from eye level.

'I think this one's slightly fuller,' he said, straightening up again and picking up the right-hand glass. 'For my guest.' And he offered it to Romola with a solemn face and a little bow. Then he raised the other glass and said: 'To absent friends.'

'Yes,' said Romola getting up from her chair and speaking with a fervour that surprised him. 'Yes. To absent friends.'

And she took a good drink from the glass and sat down again.

'I can't stay long,' she went on straight away, 'because I'll have to be getting our meal. I've come to warn you, Laurie. I think you and Brenda had better move out of here as soon as you possibly can. I'm very sorry to have to say this, but it's for your own good.'

She sat staring straight ahead of her as she spoke, not looking at him.

'I see,' said Laurie quietly. 'Or rather I think I see. Would it be something – ' He hesitated for a moment. He hated prevarication as much as Romola did, but he was a great deal younger than she was and he had a lot of respect for her and sympathy for what he suspected to be her position. Ought he to say straight out something damning about her mother, or had he better leave it to her to do so if she wished? Perhaps they could come to some understanding without her having the pain and embarrassment of making derogatory remarks about her own mother.

'It's because of my mother,' said Romola, solving his dilemma for him and earning even more of his respect. 'She's doing her best to drive a wedge between you and Brenda. It won't be the first time she's done this.'

And she proceeded to relate the story of Peter and Linda, briefly but with very telling effect.

'If you think it's incredible that two people who really love each other can be driven apart,' concluded Romola, 'I can only assure you that it is not. It's only too possible for somebody with diabolical cleverness and determination to do just that. My mother is exceedingly clever and exceedingly determined. She has no other outlets for her talents nowadays except this sort of intrigue. She has worked through all her relatives and friends and that is why she is interesting herself in comparative strangers. Unfortunately, the weaker she becomes physically, the more spiteful are her intrigues, and the cleverer she gets at concealing from people what she is really doing. Most people have no idea of what she is up to.'

'I knew,' interrupted Laurie. 'I guessed it almost at once.'

This was not strictly true, for up till today he had guessed nothing specific about Mrs Merriman. He knew only that she gave her daughter a rotten life and that he didn't trust her an inch.

'That was very perceptive of you indeed,' said Romola, turning her dark eyes upon the boy with a look of such admiration that he almost blushed. 'I knew you had some idea of what really goes on, otherwise I would not have talked to you like this. I'd have known you would never understand. Where I do blame myself is in not warning you about her before. I didn't want you and Brenda to come here at all, but unfortunately I was unable to prevent it. But I ought to have told you about her straight away. Except that you probably wouldn't have believed me. Would you have believed me, Laurie? Had you really guessed all that much?'

'I'm not sure,' admitted the boy. 'I might have thought it was you who was doing the scheming. You see, I wouldn't have known you as I do now, Miss Merriman.'

'True. Anyway, I'm warning you now. Get yourself and Brenda out of here quickly. Tomorrow. Don't leave it any later. I assure you I am not exaggerating the danger. You do believe that, don't you, Laurie?'

Again the dark eyes looked at him very intently.

He nodded. 'Yes. I know. It's rather grim. It's already started. In fact I'm afraid it's too late.'

CHAPTER VII

'Too late?'

Romola repeated the words in a quick, anxious voice. The very same words that only a short while ago Mrs Merriman had uttered in triumphant malice, Laurie was now saying with unhappiness and regret.

'She's got Brenda thoroughly hooked,' he said and proceeded, as Romola had done, to a brief but effective summary of Brenda's position vis-à-vis Patience Merriman, starting with the diary entry.

'I see,' said Romola grimly when he had finished. 'Thank you for telling me. That fills in the gaps, I think. We can guess for ourselves what sort of conversation took place between them a little while ago before Brenda went out. If I had been fully in command of myself I would have prevented that conversation, but I was not able to at that moment. I had just played right into my mother's hands by losing my temper. Brenda will have overheard me say to my mother that she didn't deserve to live. That will have clinched matters nicely. What is to be done now?'

She sat very upright in her chair and looked at him appealingly. Laurie wished with all his heart that he had something constructive to suggest, but for the moment he could think of nothing at all except that he personally would have the greatest pleasure in strangling Mrs Merriman with his own hands, crippled old woman or no crippled old woman.

'I expect you really do feel like murdering her sometimes,' was all he could find to say, and directly he had said it he thought he ought not to have done so. But again her reaction was completely sincere and totally without embarrassment or prevarication.

'I have often wished her dead,' said Romola. 'More than ever of recent years. Have I ever thought of making myself the instrument of her death?' She appeared to reflect for a moment or two. 'No. I can't truly say that I have. I don't think that means that I am too virtuous or too cowardly to consider the possibility. It is just that if you are brought up in the way I was, you simply do not think of things like killing people in connection with yourself and your own surroundings. Murders are things in books or in the newspapers.'

Even as she spoke these words, Romola heard some voice deep inside herself, right down in the depths of her mind that she had never tapped before, say to her quite clearly: 'Why not? Would it be so very wicked? If it were to save other people – not for your own benefit. You could kill her and then confess to it. Why not?'

An unfamiliar and very disturbing little voice. She was to hear more and more of it from this moment forward. But she did not mention it to Laurie.

'However,' she said aloud, making a gesture as if brushing aside this interruption of their discussion, 'that's by the way. What can we do now, that is the point, to ensure that you and Brenda don't get at cross-purposes over my mother?'

'I won't be able to get Brenda to leave here. I'm sure of

that,' said Laurie.

'Of course you won't be able to in the circumstances,' said Romola almost impatiently. 'In fact I think the only thing you can do now is to go along with her. Agree with Brenda whatever she says about my mother and myself. Do not let yourself be provoked on any account. That would be to play into her hands. But if you never rise to any bait you may keep safe. And Brenda will see straight again in time, I promise you. Do you think you can do that, Laurie? Keep it all to yourself?'

Romola looked at him doubtfully.

'I'll do my best,' said Laurie. 'I'd more or less come to the same conclusion, that that was the only thing to be done. It won't be easy.'

'You've only got to keep it up with Brenda and with my mother. If you're absolutely bursting, you can always come and talk to me. I'll be your safety valve.'

'Thanks,' said Laurie.

'Not that one can always restrain oneself, even with a safety valve,' continued Romola as if he had not spoken. 'I've had one myself for years, just in case you're afraid I have nobody to confide in. I have. But I still lose control when my mother really sets out to get at me. However, it will be Brenda you will have mainly to deal with and not my mother. That should not be quite so difficult.'

'I'm not so sure,' said Laurie slowly. 'I'm beginning to wonder whether I really know anything about Brenda at all. She's like a stranger sometimes.'

Romola's reaction to this remark took him by surprise. She got up from her armchair and came over to where he sat on an upright chair by the table and laid her hands on his shoulders and shook him a little, saying in a harsh and commanding voice: 'Stop that, Laurie! Stop it at once.

You are not to start wondering about Brenda. That's the
way the poison works. That's what you are meant to do,
can't you see? You love her. She loves you. You – must –
not – wonder. Is that clear? She will wonder. But you
mustn't. You must hold firm. Behave with her exactly
as you always have. Never, never, never give any sign at
all that you think anything is changed between you.'

She gave him another little shake.

'Have you got that clear?'

'Yes, I've got it very clear,' said Laurie, whose face
had gone very pale, and who was feeling shaken in more
ways than one.

'Then good luck.' Romola let him go and straightened
herself up. 'We must not be seen to be talking to each
other too much,' she went on, 'or they will think we are in
league together. I'm out doing a bit of gardening round
at the back most evenings between five and half past six.
If you need to speak to me, look for me there. Now I
must go. Goodbye. Be very careful indeed tonight when
Brenda comes in.'

Laurie promised again and Romola left the flat, moving
down the stairs to the first floor as quietly as she had
ascended them.

But the old woman will know that Romola has been
up to see me, said Laurie to himself. She's probably got
out of her chair and crawled up to the first floor and is
sitting in Romola's bedroom waiting to give her the
fright of her life.

He stood in the open door of the attic flat, listening for a
moment or two and half expecting to hear a little scream,
but no sound came up from the two lower floors of
Beechcroft, and when he returned to his living-room and
sat down to think about the extraordinary conversation

that he had just been having with Romola Merriman, he found himself suddenly experiencing quite a violent reaction.

Romola's warnings, that a few moments ago had struck home to him with great force because they put into more concrete form all his own half-formulated fears, now seemed to him unreal and melodramatic, something to be shaken off as one tries to rid oneself of the after-impressions of a bad dream. He looked around at the snug little room that now felt very much like home; at the posters of pre-Raphaelite ladies that he and Brenda had chosen together to brighten up the walls, at all their books and papers scattered about, and the photograph of Sam the fox terrier who had been the chief friend and mainstay of Brenda's lonely childhood, and it seemed to him quite ludicrous to imagine that anything or anybody could ever come between them.

How could the machinations of an evil old woman – and Laurie still fully believed that Mrs Merriman was that and that it gave her pleasure to try to break up other people's happiness – how could they have any effect on two people so totally committed to each other as he and Brenda were? This other young couple that Romola had talked about must have been in quite a different situation. Living together for the first time, perhaps. Trying things out. Not at all sure of themselves and very liable to be influenced by other people. He had never come across either of them during his years at Oxford. They were obviously not students from his own college or studying his own subject. Sad, of course, if the girl really had had to drop out of her degree course because of the break-up. But such things were happening all the time. Emotional upsets and broken hearts and mental breakdowns and even suicides. They happened for all sorts of reasons. Perhaps it was not Mrs Merriman's malevolence at all that had been the main cause in this particular case; perhaps there was some other factor that Romola Merriman did not know about.

While he fried himself sausages and later, while he tried without much success to concentrate on his reading, Laurie's thoughts were running intermittently on these lines. But as the time drew nearer for Brenda's return he became more and more restless and less and less able to give much attention to the rather stodgy survey of nineteenth-century legislation on education from which he was making notes. He ached for Brenda to return. He wanted and needed her more than ever.

It was as if she was already there in the room with him: a tall, sturdy girl, with a dark complexion and strong, gentle hands. A very loving and caring and conscientious girl. No raving beauty, but with thick springy black hair and a pleasant, often rather worried-looking face. It was a joy to see the worried look fade when they made love. And to see her smile, reluctantly at first, and then more broadly. Nobody had ever been able to make Brenda smile as Laurie could. He had never felt about any other girl as he did about Brenda; he would never feel like that about anyone again. He had a proposition to put to her when she returned, but meanwhile the minutes seemed very long.

And meanwhile, downstairs in the big drawing-room after a meal eaten almost in silence, Mrs Merriman interrupted a tense moment of a television crime serial to which neither she nor Romola was really paying much attention.

'It looks as if Terence is going to marry again. Won't

that be nice for him?'

There was no reaction whatever from Romola, so Mrs Merriman had to repeat the remark, much to her annoyance because these little barbs never had quite the same effect when the first one had missed fire.

'Oh? Really?' said Romola when at last the remark had sunk in.

Mrs Merriman surveyed her daughter keenly, searching for some tell-tale sign of shock or distress or self-conscious-ness, but could find none. There was no evidence of anything but complete indifference. Had she, after all, not heard what had been said? Mrs Merriman's lips began the little champing movement that always started up when she became frustrated or annoyed. She thought of repeating her comment, which was in fact pure invention, yet again, but decided against it.

A little later she tried another tactic. Shock tactics.

'Well,' she said briskly at another comparatively silent moment in the programme, while the detectives were lying spreadeagled on the roof of some sort of Nissen hut, waiting for all hell to break loose below. 'Well? Did the boy believe all the wicked tales you told him about your own mother?'

There was a little reaction this time, but less than Patience Merriman had hoped for. Romola shifted in her chair but said nothing. After settling herself into another position she relapsed once more into apparent lethargy.

In fact Romola had been prepared for this attack and had decided exactly how to meet it. Complete silence when any remark was made about Brenda or Laurie. That was to be her policy from henceforth. For there was absolutely no weapon that could be used against complete silence. Mrs Merriman worked by gaining a tiny foothold, driving in a very tiny wedge. The merest slit was enough for her. Give her that, and she would sooner or later succeed in tearing the whole fabric apart. But present a blank face and she was helpless. Romola really did not know why she had not thought of this policy before, except perhaps that it was so very difficult to keep up after her forty-eight years of always rising to the bait.

It was far from easy now, but she was going to keep it up for as long as she could. She was going to save that young couple if it was the last thing on this earth that she did. And even if in the end she had to kill her mother to save them. For the strange little voice deep within her that had first made itself heard while she talked to Laurie was getting stronger now. It was even beginning to suggest ways and means, times and places.

There was a moment of dead silence in the big drawing-room and then great bursts of gunfire came from the television screen.

'It must be rather fun,' said Romola during a temporary lull in the fake battle, 'to have one of those weapons in your hands.'

Mrs Merriman's lips chewed more vigorously than ever. Their movement had now gone quite beyond her control. She couldn't remember the last time when Romola had induced in her quite such frustration and irritation. After the wonderful triumphs of the afternoon it was particularly annoying. Romola ought at this moment to be totally beaten and cringing: instead, it looked as if she had brought up some reinforcements from some source or other and the well-tried methods of attack were failing to find their mark.

What source could it be? That boy upstairs? Mrs Merriman soon shrugged this notion off. Even if Romola had spun him a story, he would simply look on it as the fantastic ravings of a frustrated old maid. That would be the natural reaction of the young. Terence himself? Surely not. He was tightly wedged in Patience Merriman's own web. Romola would never be able to dislodge him.

Who else then?

Mrs Merriman kept as tight a watch over her daughter's activities and emotions as was possible for somebody in her condition, and she had her own sources of information. Nevertheless there were inevitably hours unaccounted for, and possibly people and events that she did not know about.

The thought that Romola could have an area of life that was outside her control caused the muscles in her face to work furiously while her mind set itself to meet this fresh challenge.

CHAPTER VIII

AT A FEW MINUTES before eleven Brenda put her bicycle into the shed and shut the door. She moved quietly as if afraid of disturbing the household, although in fact there were lights burning on every floor – in the dormer window of their bedroom at the top, in Romola's bedroom on the first floor, and in the ground-floor room where Mrs Merriman now slept and whose window looked out on the drive at the side of the house. From the strength and position of the glow that was visible through the deep pink curtains of this room, Brenda judged that there was nothing but the bedside lamp burning, which meant that the old lady would be in bed waiting for her.

It was comforting to know that she was so eagerly expected and to know that she herself was about to give somebody else comfort. For Brenda's last evening at the snack bar had been a particularly miserable one. The smell and the heat had been worse than ever and the manageress had sworn at her and made unpleasant remarks about the youth of today when she said she would not be coming back, although in fact she was only employed by the hour and was not obliged to give any longer notice. The only comfort was that the argument with Laurie in her mind had died down at last, and as she put her latchkey noiselessly into the lock of the wide front door of Beechcroft, Brenda was thinking entirely about Mrs Merriman and not about Laurie at all.

Two floors up Laurie, having heard the faint sound of the gate for which he had been waiting eagerly the past half hour, stuck his head out of the dormer window in the hope of catching a glimpse of Brenda on the doorstep. The roof tiles and the guttering blocked his view, but in any case it was a dark night and the light outside the front door had not been switched on.

Laurie drew back and shut the window again and hugged himself in an agony of impatience to have Brenda there so that he could tell her how much he loved her and put to her the plans he had been making for their future.

One minute, two minutes, three minutes . . .

Brenda was taking an incredibly long time to come upstairs. The boy's arms fell to his sides and a very worried expression came over his face. He went and stood in the open doorway of the top-floor flat and listened and listened.

'Shut the door, dear,' murmured Mrs Merriman to

Brenda, 'and come close to me. That's right. I don't suppose my daughter is actually eavesdropping, but we can't be too careful.'

Mrs Merriman was wearing a pink nightgown tied high round the neck and round the wrists with pink ribbons. The fine white hair was fluffy round her face and her eyes looked up at the girl pleadingly. How strange, thought Brenda yet again, that somebody so old and weak could really look quite pretty.

But she also looked very defenceless and rather frightened. As Brenda pulled up a chair to the head of the bed she noticed that on the little table where the reading lamp stood there also stood a cup and saucer, and in the cup was some sort of milky drink that had been allowed to go cold.

'Didn't you want your hot drink?' asked Brenda as she sat down.

Mrs Merriman's hands gripped the bedclothes. 'I daren't drink it,' she whispered. 'Romola brought it to me. I'm so afraid she's put something in it.'

'Oh dear.' It came as something of a shock to Brenda to realize the practical implications of suspecting that somebody under your own roof was thinking of murdering you. 'Would she do that, do you think?' she added rather feebly.

Mrs Merriman controlled a surge of impatience. 'I don't know,' she said, still in the same low and frightened voice, 'but I daren't drink it.'

'Would you like me to get you some warm milk?' asked Brenda, since this seemed to be what she was intended to say.

'That would be so very kind,' said Mrs Merriman. 'I'm supposed to take a tablet, you see, with a hot drink last thing at night, but after this afternoon . . . I don't know what I'm going to do.' Her voice was almost tearful. 'I am so very helpless.'

Brenda fussed over her and tried to soothe her, re-arranging the pillows, which had been perfectly comfortable, into a shape that was less comfortable. Mrs Merriman had more and more difficulty in controlling herself. The tears that now flowed freely from her eyes were the result of frustration and annoyance, not of weakness and fear. But they were very real tears all the same and they served their purpose even better than Mrs Merriman had hoped. Brenda's mother had wept frequently after quarrels with Brenda's father, and the girl had not always shown the sympathy she felt she ought to have shown. Laurie had been patiently working on what he considered to be Brenda's irrational guilt feelings towards her mother and had had some success, all of which was undone now as the old guilt feelings were stirred up afresh by the sight of the old woman's tears.

'Don't cry, Mrs Merriman, please don't cry,' murmured Brenda. 'I'll look after you. You don't need to worry. I'll make sure you come to no harm. I'll get your milk now, shall I? Do you have Ovaltine or anything like that in it?'

'No, thank you,' quavered the old lady. 'Just milk. And a little sugar.'

Strong emotion of any kind is catching, and Brenda crept across the hall and into the kitchen with as much nervous caution as if she had been burgling the house. She dared not put a light on, and in the little light that came from the slightly open door of Mrs Merriman's bedroom the hall and staircase looked shadowy and sinister. It was a relief to get into the kitchen and shut the door behind her and switch on the light. But having done that, Brenda stood blinking in the sudden glare of the strip lighting, holding the cup which was spilling its unsavoury-looking contents into the saucer, and momentarily feeling quite at a loss.

At the best of times there is something a little daunting about somebody else's kitchen, with its blank cupboard doors containing anything from old saucepans to the best crockery, and its cooker with little habits of its own, and the nervous feeling in the intruder of doing things in a manner which the owner of the kitchen would disapprove, and putting things into the wrong places.

Brenda, a domesticated girl by nature, had all of these sensations on top of her present physical weariness and mental confusion. She could not possibly desert Mrs Merriman now, but on the other hand it was high time she went upstairs to Laurie, because he must be wondering why on earth she was taking so long to come upstairs. And when she did see Laurie this awful argument was surely going to take place, and she simply could not face it at the moment.

It was a big old-fashioned kitchen, well-equipped with modern gadgets, and with a big window overlooking the garden at the back. Romola and her mother frequently had their meals there now that the former dining-room had been converted into Mrs Merriman's bedroom. Brenda took a few steps towards the sink, clutching the cup and saucer with both hands, and trying to get a firmer mental grip on herself so that she could weigh up the position she had got herself into in this strange household.

The last thing that occurred to her at this moment was to taste or smell the congealed milk drink to try to find out whether or not it had been drugged in some way. She was still moving in a slow and hesitant manner in the direction of the sink when a slight sound behind her caused her to start violently, spilling much of the sticky liquid on to the floor as she turned round.

'Hullo, Brenda,' said Romola in what the girl felt to be a quietly menacing manner. 'Is there anything the matter?'

'You startled me,' said Brenda setting the tilted cup right way up again.

'You startled me too,' said Romola with a faint smile. 'I didn't expect to find anyone here in the kitchen.'

'I'm awfully sorry,' said Brenda, averting her eyes from the dark ones that were staring at her with such strange and frightening intensity. 'It's only that your mother ...'

She could not go on. How could one possibly say outright, 'I am getting some fresh milk for your mother because she's afraid you might have poisoned this cup'? She looked down at the few remaining dregs and at the sticky liquid now making a great pool on the blue-patterned linoleum, and for the first time felt that she ought to have tried to check whether it was poisoned or not. Laurie would have known immediately that that was the right thing to do. A great revulsion at the whole business came over her, and at that moment she wished herself and Laurie right out of it, miles away from the pleasant little flat that they had been so happy to make into their first real home, miles away, anywhere, making do in any filthy and crowded old place, anything so long as Beechcroft and its owners were well and truly out of their lives.

The moment of revulsion came to an end when Romola spoke again.

'I suppose my mother asked you to get her some fresh milk,' she said. 'It looks as if she had let her drink go cold. I'm so sorry you've been troubled, Brenda. You must be longing to go to bed. Don't worry about my mother. I'll see to her.'

And she held out her hand for the cup, but Brenda still clung to it.

'I think I'd better get it,' she muttered awkwardly. 'She specially wanted me to bring it to her.'

She glanced up at the older woman and caught a flash of some strong and alarming emotion in the face, quickly brought under control again.

'All right then,' said Romola, moving towards the sink and opening a cupboard at the side. 'Here's the saucepans. The cooker lights itself and the front burners are the quickest. My mother likes Ovaltine best, with about half a teaspoon of sugar. And if you want to mop up the floor, here's a cloth.'

She spoke in a detached and aloof manner, rather as if she were the lady of the house showing a raw young domestic recruit how to do the job. Even in her present confused state Brenda recognized the tone and resented it. She had some experience of being casually and even rudely treated in her various vacation jobs, but this was different. It was at this moment that she switched over from merely thinking Romola Merriman rather odd, odd enough even to be a murderer, to positively disliking her.

'Thanks for telling me where things are,' she said. 'I shall need to know that if I am going to look after Mrs

Merriman. Naturally I'll wipe the floor.'

Again there came that flash of a violent emotion into Romola's face, but she said no more until she had her hand on the door-handle. There she paused for a moment and looked straight at Brenda.

'My mother has a bell by the side of her bed that rings in my room,' she said. 'If she needs help in the night she rings this bell. I thought you might like to know this. Good night.'

And she left the room.

Brenda wiped the floor, washed the cup and saucer, and poured milk into a saucepan, all with quick and angry movements. She was a girl who was easily worried but normally slow to anger, and the sort of resentment she was now feeling was very strange to her. That Romola's seeming coolness and arrogance could be due to intense embarrassment never entered Brenda's head. She was not, as Laurie knew well, endowed with very much imagination.

Mrs Merriman was tearfully grateful when Brenda brought the hot drink. She asked the girl to tip out one of her tablets for her and to help her sit up while she drank. It was a relief to be asked to perform straightforward and simple little actions. Brenda did all this most willingly and decided that she would not mention that Romola had been downstairs unless Mrs Merriman mentioned it herself.

When the old lady had finished drinking, she clung to Brenda's hand and begged her to sit by her bed a little, just until the drug began to work and she was on the way to falling asleep.

'It's ever so silly of me,' she murmured. 'I'm being a terrible nuisance to you, I know. But it would be such a kindness. You're so sensible and strong and reliable. I can't tell you what it means to me, knowing that you are here.'

Brenda turned the lamplight away from the bed, sat down in the chair again, and laid a hand on one of the old lady's as it lay on the bedcover. Laurie will just have to lump it if I don't come up just yet, she said to herself. I can't possibly leave her. He must see that. In any case he's probably asleep by now.

At the top of the house Laurie at last heard footsteps on the stairs. He rushed out eagerly and saw Romola in a crimson dressing-gown coming slowly up from the first floor. Disappointment and anxiety fought in him for the upper hand.

'What's happening?' he whispered.

She made a little helpless gesture. 'It looks as if Mother has Brenda in there for the night,' she whispered back. 'We'd better not interfere just yet. It's wiser to let things ride. If she comes up later you must be very careful indeed, Laurie. Remember you promised.'

'I haven't forgotten,' he said, feeling suddenly very flat and cold at heart after his recent impatient anxiety.

CHAPTER IX

THE NEXT FEW DAYS were nightmarish to Laurie. He could scarcely have felt worse if Brenda had walked out on him or if they had had a violent quarrel. But they had no such quarrel, partly owing to tremendous efforts of self-control on his side, and partly owing to the fact that he saw so little of her.

On the night after she had first become 'bewitched' as
Laurie mentally called it, Brenda came upstairs at about
2 a.m. and went straight to the bathroom, where Laurie
heard running water. He did not call out to her: safer
perhaps to let her make the first move. After a little while
she came into the bedroom and got into the other one
of the two single beds that they had pushed together.
She did not switch on the light and she moved very
stealthily as if trying not to disturb him.

Laurie lay tense and waiting, making no move, every
bit of him aching to welcome her with all his heart and
all his love. If they had indeed had a violent quarrel,
this was what he would have done. But it was so much
worse than a quarrel: it was like an endless tunnel of
unspoken misunderstanding, a vast uncharted quicksand
into which they had both stumbled.

He turned over and reached out an arm and said in a
sleepy voice as if he had just woken up: 'Hullo, darling.
What's the time?'

Surely that was innocuous and could provoke no storm.

'Very late,' replied Brenda in a low, strained voice.
'Sorry I woke you.'

And she curled up as she always did when falling asleep,
like some wild animal finding sanctuary at last against all
the dangers of the world, and said no more.

It didn't need Romola's advice for him to realize that
it was wisest to leave Brenda alone for the time being.
Towards dawn, after one of the most agonized nights he
had spent for a long time, Laurie fell asleep at last.

When he awoke, Brenda had gone. But she had written
him a note, and that gave him a little glimmer of hope
that had to last a long time. There were no particular

expressions of affection in it, but at least she had thought enough about him to let him know what was happening and the note was not unfriendly.

'I'm going to look after Mrs Merriman for a while. As a job,' she wrote. 'We've not yet decided whether she'll pay me a wage or whether she'll reduce the rent or waive it completely. I'll let you know what we arrange. I'm getting all her meals for her and she likes an early breakfast in bed. I shan't be going back to the snack bar. If I don't see you before you go, have a good day. Hope you get some nice tourist parties.'

It was written in Brenda's small tight handwriting at the top of a large sheet of lined paper torn from the looseleaf pad on which she made her study notes, and Laurie found it lying flat on the table in their kitchen. He read it again and again as he sat drinking one cup of coffee after another to try to rouse himself enough to face the day.

In a few minutes he had the contents of the note by heart but he continued to read it none the less. The more he pondered over the words while trying to hold in his mind the vision of his own Brenda, the more he saw of bewilderment and strain in her own mind and the less of any coolness or ill will towards himself. Don't take it personally, he said to himself again and again. Try to think that she's having a sort of nervous breakdown.

He used these same words to Romola a little later. She had taken the car out of the garage and was checking the oil when he came to collect his bicycle from the shed. They talked in whispers, although Mrs Merriman's bedroom window was shut and it was scarcely possible for them to be overheard from the house.

'She's working something out of herself,' said Laurie. 'It's probably this guilt thing she's got about her own mother.'

Romola agreed. 'You just hold on to that,' she said as she let the bonnet of the big Austin fall back into place, 'and don't let her talk to you about my mother at all. You're doing fine so far. And Laurie – '

It was a harsh whisper now. There were shadows under her eyes and her face looked old and strained as if she too had scarcely slept.

'Yes?' He swung his bike round and banged a hand on the saddle. Anybody chancing to see them would surely think they were exchanging the briefest morning greeting. 'At least it's stopped raining for once,' Laurie added, glancing up at the sky.

Romola picked up a rag and began to wipe over the windscreen of the car. When her head came within a yard of Laurie's she said in the same low voice, filled with emotion: 'It won't be for long. I'm going to do something about it. It's gone on long enough, this poisoning of other people's lives. I'm putting a stop to it once and for all.'

She moved round the front of the car to rub the other side of the windscreen and called out brightly: 'Have a good day. Looks as if we might even get some sunshine.'

'See you,' said Laurie, and scooted off down the drive.

He had heard and seen nothing whatever of either Brenda or of Mrs Merriman. Presumably they were closeted together in the latter's bedroom, because the door had been closed when he came through the hall and the doors of all the other ground-floor rooms had been open. Had she been at the window of the bedroom, he wondered, keeping out of sight behind the curtains, but watching him put one foot on the pedal and give a kick that sent him the whole length of the drive, as he always did? It comforted him just a little to think that she might have watched him depart, but Romola's last words, which were no doubt intended to encourage and reassure him, in fact did no such thing.

'It's gone on long enough, this poisoning people's lives . . . I'm putting a stop to it . . .'

How could she be putting a stop to it, Laurie asked himself as he pedalled along the Woodstock Road, except by taking very drastic action? It was obvious that neither Romola nor anybody else had the least control over Mrs Merriman. You could no more argue or reason with that wicked old woman than you could with a raging lioness or a viper. She had no better feelings to appeal to and if you tried to threaten her it was simply playing into her own hands, playing her own game, increasing the grip of her tentacles on poor Brenda.

Of course Romola knew all this, so if she said she was going to put a stop to it she must have something very drastic in mind. Laurie heartily wished he could not so easily guess what that 'something' might be. Everything he had come to know about Romola Merriman – and since yesterday afternoon he felt he had come to know her pretty well – pointed to her being a woman of unusual strength of character. Seemingly the victim and tool of her mother, she yet possessed great hidden resources. If that mother had been a good woman suffering from an agonizing and incurable disease, Romola was the sort of person who would take the law into her own hands and carry out a mercy killing.

In fact it would be a sort of mercy killing if indeed she were planning murder now. Merciful for Laurie and for

Brenda and for anybody else whose lives Mrs Merriman
might try to wreck.

Not to mention for Romola herself, but Laurie felt sure
that her own release was the last thing that was concerning
her. If Romola Merriman was really planning to kill her
mother then it was surely from the most unselfish of
motives.

But if she was planning it, would she have dropped such
a very broad hint to Laurie, however much she felt the
urge to reassure him and bring him hope?

The whole business was worrying in the extreme. To
think that somebody you liked and admired might be
planning murder on your behalf was as bad if not worse
than knowing that somebody was deliberately alienating
your girl from you.

Laurie parked his bike near the Martyrs' Memorial,
padlocked it, and walked the couple of hundred yards to
the tourist office that was employing him on an hourly
basis to take groups of visitors round Oxford. He was good
at the job, being at the same time knowledgeable but not
too boringly informative, and there was usually plenty
for him to do. With the improvement in the weather he
was kept busy all day, and had little leisure to dwell on
what was happening at Beechcroft. At one time, having
expatiated at some length to his flock on the beauties of
the High Street, he led them into the narrow pedestrian
way of Magpie Lane and then brought them to an abrupt
halt.

'You are now standing,' he said in a mock-serious voice,
'upon the most significant spot in the whole city of
Oxford.'

Two elderly American couples, four Japanese of in-
determinate age, two French teenagers, and two other

young people who wore the worldwide blue denim uniform of modern youth and might have come from anywhere, stopped obediently on the flagstones and stared up at an excessively high stone wall over which was drooping a magnificent horse-chestnut tree.

The American faces composed themselves once more into expressions of reverential interest; the Japanese began to position their expensive cameras; and the young people looked at Laurie expectantly, puzzled but quite confident that this boy who was in appearance so much like themselves would not let them down.

'It was exactly here,' said Laurie, moving about half a yard to the left, 'that I first ran into my girl-friend. I really did run into her. I was cycling along here which I shouldn't have been doing and she side-stepped to the wrong side to avoid me and I knocked all her books and lecture notes flying. We spent ages picking them all up.'

His audience laughed and chatted and even the most footsore of the American ladies thought what a nice boy he was, not a bit standoffish and superior as you might expect an Oxford student to be, but perfectly ordinary and friendly. One of the Japanese managed to say, in barely comprehensible English, that it must have been a very romantic meeting, and the unidentifiable youngsters wanted to know what his girl-friend was like, what she was studying, and whether there was any prejudice against women at Oxford.

Laurie responded to them all, but it cost him an enormous effort to do so, and he heartily wished he had not brought in this little piece of light relief that always went down well with the weary sightseers and refreshed them before the long drag round Christ Church. For the moment he had finished this little anecdote, one of the several little personal stories that he brought in to enliven the endless recital of founders of colleges and doings of famous men, he had found himself overcome with the blackest of depressions. It affected him physically, both his eyesight and his hearing. It was as if a mist had come and blotted out the sun, which had at last struggled through and was turning to light gold the warm yellow-grey stones of the college buildings at the end of the narrow lane in which they stood. And the questions and comments of the little group of tourists seemed to come from a great distance and to be as meaningless as the chatter of monkeys.

It was quite true, what he had said about his first meeting with Brenda. That was exactly what had happened. After collecting all her scattered papers he had of course offered to treat her to a coffee in recompense, and in the little café in St Aldates where he now proposed to take his charges for tea, they had had the first of the many long talks in which they came to know and understand each other so well and to realize how much they could do for each other. Brenda needed Laurie's liveliness and Laurie needed Brenda's deeply caring nature. They fitted. They were right for each other. And it had got better and better as the months went by, until at last they were a part of one another, neither one of them any longer complete alone, and that was how it had stayed for the next two years, while they had lived sometimes apart and sometimes together, in their respective colleges and in various communal student houses, until Terence Toogood had told Laurie that he had found the perfect accommodation for them – a self-contained furnished flat at an incredibly cheap rent, in the household of the widow of the famous Professor Francis Merriman.

'Oh yes, some of the colleges are mixed,' said Laurie, answering a question from one of the French teenagers. 'In fact most of the men's colleges now take women too. But the women's colleges don't seem so keen on taking men. What do you make of that?'

Again there was a laugh.

'Shall we go on?' said Laurie. 'If we go along here – this is Bear Lane – we come out to St Aldates where we can get some tea before we tackle Christ Church. That's the back of it down there, but it's a great barracks of a place and there's a hell of a lot to see. Don't you think tea first would be a good idea?'

Most of the party, including the youngsters, thought a tea-break would be a very good idea. Only one of the indefatigable Japanese looked as if he was ready to proceed immediately to the business of covering the largest and possibly the most spectacular of all the colleges of Oxford.

'Oh no, it's not my own college,' said Laurie as he shepherded his party along some more narrow thoroughfares. 'Mine's much smaller. And much more select of course.'

The afternoon wore on, and everywhere he went Laurie took with him this great black cloud of depression that turned this lovely city that he loved so much and hoped to make his home into a ghost town, and he heard his own voice as if from a long way off, endlessly talking, quoting dates, names, anecdotes, cracking silly jokes, answering the same endless questions.

CHAPTER X

THE NEXT DAY passed in much the same manner for Laurie. The sun continued to shine intermittently. An ever-changing series of faces – white, brown, and yellow – asked the never-changing questions and made the same remarks. His own voice went on and on, telling the same little stories. But he never told the story of how he had first met Brenda again. It was too painful.

When he got back to Beechcroft he felt an over-whelming revulsion at the thought of going into the house at all. The iron gates and the standard rose-bushes and the red brick that even its surrounding copper beeches and chestnut trees could not mellow were all as hateful and menacing to him as if the place were a prison. But within those walls were not only all his own material possessions, including his most treasured books, but also the human being who mattered more to him than anyone else in the world.

She's a silly girl and I love her, said Laurie to himself as he put away his bike, casually and carelessly now, no longer with any spirits to do his bowling act. She's not even all that pretty but I love her. Nor all that brainy. Nor all that anything. But I love her.

He shut the door of the shed and walked round to the back garden. This mental cataloguing of Brenda's failings was, if anything, making him feel even worse. He didn't really want to talk to Romola at this moment, in fact he didn't want to do anything but hide away and howl to himself, but that had been the arrangement, that he should meet her in the back garden at about this time.

She was down at the far end, in the vegetable patch behind the screen of climbing red roses. Just standing there staring at the runner-beans, with no watering-can or gardening tools, doing nothing at all. She was even wearing her blue linen frock, most unsuitable for gardening, and the look on her face, of which Laurie caught a glimpse before she saw him, filled him with a mixture of pity and alarm.

But a moment later he began to feel angry with her. Quite irrationally, because it was not Romola who had brought him to his present miserable condition. In fact he genuinely believed that she was going to all lengths to bring this condition to an end, but unhappiness finds fault everywhere, and Romola was an integral part of this horrible household and therefore of Laurie's unhappiness.

'What's happening?' he asked abruptly, without any other greeting.

'It's awful for you, Laurie,' she said in a voice full of warmth and sympathy. 'But it won't last much longer. I promise you. Just keep on as you are. You're doing wonderfully well.'

He looked away from her and kicked a stone from the path into the raspberry bushes. The neighbour's cat shot out with a startled yelp and leapt over the fence.

'I'm not doing anything. I've barely seen her,' muttered Laurie.

'That's all that's needed,' said Romola. 'See her as little as you can and it will all come out right in the end.' She took a step towards him and laid both hands on his arm. 'It's going to be all right, Laurie. You and Brenda are going to come through this. I promise you.'

'But how – ' Laurie broke off and swallowed. 'I mean, what can you do? What are you going to do?'

'I can't tell you that. I can only promise you that my mother will get her claws off Brenda. You've got to believe me. Please believe me.'

It really was a very beautiful voice. And the eyes were still beautiful too, even more startling than ever in that pale tense face. Laurie found himself wondering what she had looked like a quarter of a century ago, before he had been born. She was an extraordinary woman, even now. But then she had extraordinary parents, both of them, in their very different ways.

'I just hope you're not doing anything too – ' He paused. 'Anything too drastic.'

'There was something rather drastic happened this afternoon,' said Romola with a faint smile. 'You will no doubt hear about it. But remember. No comment. Don't argue with anything that may be said to you.'

'I'll remember,' said Laurie.

But when he came into the house, he found all the doors on the ground floor closed, and there was no sound of voices from behind any of them. The only sign that anybody was about was the smell of boiling chicken coming from the kitchen. Presumably Brenda was getting the meal. Controlling the impulse to peep in and say hullo to her, Laurie ran upstairs to the attic flat. What he found there raised his spirits considerably.

Lying on the kitchen table, alongside a basin covered over with foil, was a note from Brenda. And it actually started off with 'Darling Laurie'.

'This only needs heating,' it went on. 'I made a bit extra stew at lunch-time for you and there's potatoes in the saucepan. Sorry I can't have it with you, but Mrs

Merriman wants me to do all the cooking because . . . well, you can guess why. Hope you had a good day and I'll get up to have coffee with you if I can. TT is coming in for coffee this evening so I might be able to get away for a bit. Lots of love. B.'

Laurie picked up the basin containing the stew and held it precariously in one hand while he danced a little jig round the kitchen.

'Good for you, Romola,' he cried aloud when he came to a stop. 'You're right. Dead right. It works.'

And he ate with far greater appetite than he had ever expected to summon up again. Of course it was working, he told himself as he ate the raspberries that Brenda had left for him too – or was it Romola who had put them there? – of course it worked because the surest way to be first in Brenda's thoughts was to have her feel guilty about you, and there was no doubt that she was feeling very guilty towards Laurie, and with good cause.

Romola had realized that. She had summed up Brenda. That wicked old Mrs Merriman was not the only one who understood how people functioned and how to work on them. Her daughter understood it too, but she would use her insight for benevolent purposes and not for evil.

Laurie's recovered joy in life swung him right over to the far end of the pendulum, almost into a state of euphoria. Even the fear that Romola might be planning to kill her mother, that had been reinforced yet again by her remarks in the vegetable garden, began to fade away. Perhaps he had completely misunderstood. Perhaps when she had said that it would not be long, all she had meant was that it would not take long for Brenda to come to her senses and see what Mrs Merriman was

really like, provided they were both allowed to get on
with it uninterrupted so to speak. Leave them alone.
Give the old girl enough rope to hang herself. Give her no
opposition and she would be helpless. In other words,
keep out of the way, Romola, keep out of the way,
Laurie.

Surely it must be nothing more sinister than that that
Romola had in mind?

But if so, then why had she not taken him fully into her
confidence and told him so?

By the time he heard Brenda's footsteps on the attic
stairs, Laurie's mind had come into a state of balance
again, and he had decided that Romola was, after all,
intending to do something more drastic than simply
letting things take their course. For in fact all that had
really been gained by his own self-restraint was that
Brenda felt guilty towards him and was therefore treating
him more kindly. Which was wonderful as far as it went
and it had been a tonic to his spirits, but the essential
situation remained unchanged. And no doubt the old
woman had all sorts of tricks up her sleeve, ready to
cope with any little sign of weakening on Brenda's part.

Coming back to a state of equilibrium after a state of
euphoria is very nearly as bad as sinking from a normal
condition into the depths of depression. It is the drop that
is so painful, and so by the time Brenda came into the
flat, Laurie actually felt low in spirits again and it was
this that caused him to make his mistake.

It did not happen immediately. The first thing that
happened was that Brenda rushed into his arms and
clung to him. Then she asked him whether he had
enjoyed his supper and his reply led to a fresh display of
emotion. It was almost like old times but his hopes were

dashed when she said, in answer to his unspoken question: 'I'll have to sleep downstairs, darling. It's a bore but I don't see how it can be avoided. She's terrified to be left alone at night. We've made up a bed on the big settee in the sitting-room and we'll leave both the doors open so that I can hear if she needs me.'

Laurie's spirits went down with an almost audible plop. But all he said was: 'All right. I quite understand. I hope you'll be comfortable enough and will get some sleep.'

'Oh, I shall be comfy,' said Brenda. 'Don't worry about me. If I can manage to creep up some time during the night . . .'

Up shot Laurie's emotional thermometer a couple of points.

'. . . then I will,' said Brenda, 'but I don't think it's very likely. I'd never forgive myself if something happened to her while I was up here with you. You do understand, don't you, Laurie?'

And her grey eyes, almost on a level with his own and very much the same colour as his, looked at him with troubled appeal.

'Of course I understand, love,' he said. 'I know exactly how you feel. As if I didn't know you!'

She smiled faintly and they kissed again and it was then that he made his mistake. This coming together again had weakened his guard. The temptation to cement the reunion, to prove that they were in fact of much the same opinion after all, was momentarily irresistible to Laurie.

'As a matter of fact, I'm beginning to think you might be right,' he said.

'Oh Laurie!'

She drew back a little. She looked surprised, troubled,

agitated, but not pleased, and he knew at once that it had all gone wrong, that the little devil that had prompted him to make that remark was going to triumph.

'But we'd better not talk about it,' he added hastily. 'Least said soonest mended, to coin a phrase.'

This desperate effort to remedy the error by levity met with no success.

'I haven't mentioned it to you again,' said Brenda with ever increasing agitation, 'because I didn't want us to quarrel and I was so afraid that we would if we talked about it. But if you agree with me, then that's quite different. Oh Laurie!' – and she held him in a convulsive grip – 'you can't think how awful it's been! Having to keep watch every moment. Knowing that it's up to you and you alone to prevent a murder!'

Laurie held her and said nothing. He could not trust himself to speak. Love and pity for Brenda were struggling with a sense of great disgust at his own disloyalty to Romola. What on earth had induced him to think it would bring him closer to Brenda if he let her know that he too suspected Romola of planning to kill her mother? They would still see it from completely different viewpoints and the gulf between them would be as wide as ever. You might as well say that it would resolve an argument between a colour-blind person and one with normal vision if they could only agree that the object under discussion was really there. Of course it didn't settle anything. It only meant that they disagreed over the colour of the object instead.

If only he had held his tongue! In silence lay safety, as Romola had known so well. Once start talking to Brenda about Mrs Merriman's fears, whether or not he believed they might be justified, and they would be quarrelling in no time. Laurie could see that now only too plainly. But it was too late, because Brenda was already talking. And what she had to say was really very alarming indeed.

CHAPTER XI

'IT WAS A NEAR MISS this afternoon,' said Brenda, settling down in her usual armchair.

'What was, darling?' asked Laurie, propping himself on the arm and preparing to listen but to say nothing, whatever the provocation. This would be the drastic happening that Romola had referred to so briefly and that he must on no account comment on, whatever it might turn out to be.

'She wouldn't go out for a drive with Romola,' said Brenda, 'even though I offered to come too, because she was so afraid Romola would deliberately crash the car.'

'But that would kill or injure them both,' objected Laurie, immediately breaking his good resolution.

'She wouldn't mind risking that,' said Brenda with great bitterness. 'And she wouldn't mind risking my life either. Anyway, it's usually the driver who survives a crash if anyone does. But Mrs Merriman wouldn't go. She said she wouldn't dream of letting me put myself into any danger.'

Laurie's private and very rude comment on this statement remained unspoken.

'So Romola said she'd go on her own,' continued Brenda. 'They've got some stuff for a jumble sale that some people they know at Iffley are running, and she suggested that her mother might like the drive.'

'So what happened?' asked Laurie in the rather long pause that followed this statement.

'Mrs Merriman said to me that she would love to get a little air and see something of the outside world for a change, now that the weather had improved at last, and I suggested that I should push her chair and take her out that way. I wouldn't have minded going to the Parks, but she said it was too far for me, and that if we just went round the block that would be enough.'

Again Brenda paused but this time Laurie said nothing. Better get into practice for the restraint that was no doubt going to be demanded of him any moment now.

'I'd got the chair down the steps and down the path and was nearly at the front gate,' said Brenda. 'Actually it's very easy to push and no effort at all. Romola had gone off to put the stuff for the jumble sale in the car and she had just got in and was going to drive out of the gates when I'd got Mrs Merriman to where the path joins the drive. You know where I mean?'

'Yes,' said Laurie, who was beginning to get a strong suspicion of where this narrative was leading.

'Then Mrs Merriman said, "Oh dear, I've gone and forgotten my sunglasses – if it stays bright as this I'm going to need them – so would you mind fetching them for me?" So naturally I said I'd fetch them and I said I wouldn't be a minute and left her there, just at the end of the path. She could see where the car was and Romola could see perfectly well where she was. And the moment my back was turned Romola drove the car straight at her.'

'Just a minute,' said Laurie, feeling that it was so important to get at the truth of this that it was worth taking the risk of going against Romola's advice and asking some questions, 'if your back was turned you didn't actually see anything, did you? I'm not doubting you for one moment, darling. I'm just trying to get the picture. You know me. Always needing additional evidence.'

Brenda ignored this and Laurie sensed the restraint in her voice when she continued.

'I knew you wouldn't want to believe it, in spite of what you said just now. I didn't want to believe it either. It was pretty horrible. It gave me an awful shock as well.'

'Darling!'

'I heard the engine start up when I'd got to the front door,' said Brenda, wriggling away from his consolatory embrace, 'but I didn't look round immediately because I didn't realize what she was going to do. I thought she was just going to drive straight out – if I thought anything at all. She was in a filthy temper and couldn't be away from us quick enough.'

Again Laurie smothered his own private comment.

'I looked round when I heard the brakes screeching,' continued Brenda, 'but even then I didn't realize for a moment. I thought Romola had shot out of the drive without looking and had had to stop suddenly because of a car in the road. But she hadn't got as far as the gates. The car was skidded sideways across the drive with the bonnet knocking into the rose-bush at the end of the path and Mrs Merriman's chair was right out in the drive by the front gate. It was still upright and she was still in it, but it was out of control and she was trying to stop it rolling out into the road.'

Brenda glanced at him to see what impression she was making. Laurie had not the slightest doubt that it had all looked exactly as she had said. Brenda was as thorough, as observant, and as honest a witness as any court of law could hope to find. Nothing and nobody would ever be able to shake her on any point of fact. But the interpretation of these facts was quite another matter.

It seemed to him that Romola was perfectly capable of driving a car at Mrs Merriman with intent to do her harm. It also seemed to him quite possible that Romola would do this with no thought of the consequences to herself; that if she saw the chance of killing her mother she might well take it, however many witnesses there were, and in the absolute certainty that she was going to be convicted of the deed. But what he did not believe was that Romola would make a hash of the job if that was what she had decided to do. She would not attempt it unless she was quite sure it was going to work, and she would carry it through. It would not be a half-hearted and abortive attempt like this: it would be the real thing. And she would certainly not have spoken to him as she had done in the garden, had she made an unsuccessful attempt to kill her mother only a couple of hours before.

This was his deep conviction, but he had nothing to back it up except what he believed to be his own knowledge of the people concerned, and the very last thing he must do now was to let Brenda know what he suspected had really happened. This was, of course, that Mrs Merriman had deliberately arranged for Brenda to leave her in the chair just where the path from the front door joined the drive, at the very moment when Romola was about to drive out, and that she had then manoeuvred the chair forward into the path of the car so that Romola had to brake violently to avoid hitting her. This would have resulted in the very tableau that Brenda had described;

but unless there happened to be a witness to the incident as reliable as Brenda herself and with the additional advantage of being quite unbiased, Laurie did not see how it could possibly be proved one way or another. The notorious difficulty of getting at the truth in cases of road accidents gave him very little hope.

No one else but Mrs Merriman and her daughter would ever know what had really happened, and even then there was room for error. The old lady would no doubt say, if challenged, that the chair went out of her control; Romola would say that she did not expect the chair to move. One or the other, or neither of them, would be believed according to where the sympathies of their audience lay.

What then was to be done? To say as little as possible, as Romola had advised. But Brenda would be suspicious if he showed no further interest at all. In fact she was becoming suspicious already and he really must make some sort of comment.

'It must have been a frightful shock for you,' he said very seriously. 'What happened next? I hope Mrs Merriman wasn't hurt.'

'She wasn't actually injured,' replied Brenda, 'but she was very shaken and she asked me to send for the doctor.'

'What about Romola?'

'Oh, she got out of the car and pretended to be very worried and I must say I think her mother behaved extremely well, considering what had just happened. She didn't accuse Romola at all, but I could tell by the way she was clinging to me how scared she was, and later on she did say to me that she thought it might have been done on purpose and what a lucky escape she'd had.'

'It was very lucky,' agreed Laurie slowly. That was

true, he thought, whichever interpretation you put on it, because if Mrs Merriman had done what he believed she had, then she had been taking a great risk, for Romola might easily have been unable to stop the car in time. The old woman certainly had courage, he thought; you'd got to hand her that. But that made her all the more dangerous. If she was ready to risk her life and perhaps even deliberately to lose her life in order to incriminate her daughter, it looked only too likely that she would succeed. Especially if the daughter was determined to let her succeed.

Laurie was torn between a longing to be right out of it all and let them get on with it and an equally strong longing not to let either of them get away with it; to rescue Romola from her mother and to get rid of Mrs Merriman without Romola having to be sacrificed as well. Neither of these feelings could be mentioned to Brenda. He and she were very close together now, actually sitting on the same chair, but their thoughts and their feelings could hardly have been further apart. It was new to him and peculiarly unpleasant, this combination of physical proximity and mental estrangement. He wondered if Brenda was conscious of it too.

'What did you tell the doctor?' he asked.

'Only that it was an accident. That her hand had slipped and she let the chair roll down the slope. Mrs Merriman didn't want me to say anything else, and he didn't ask any questions. I suppose he might have suspected something, but he didn't say so. Not when I was there anyway.'

'Which doctor do they have?'

'Forrest. Dr Geoffrey Forrest. He comes to the student health centre sometimes. I've seen him there once or twice and he actually remembered me.'

'I know him too!' cried Laurie quite excitedly. 'It was before we met. In my first term. I had an insane ambition to become a rugger blue – God knows why – and I'd sprained a wrist. I'm sure he was the man I saw. Tall and thin and rather elegant. Sixtyish.'

'That's right,' said Brenda.

'I liked him. He behaved like his age. Didn't pretend to be matey and with-it and all up to date with the youth of today. In fact it was he who talked Jan out of the abortion. Or rather he didn't talk her out of it at all but promised to arrange it, but somehow or other by the time she'd seen him a couple of times and taken Alan along to see him too it turned into them not only deciding to keep the baby but actually getting married.'

Laurie laughed with genuine pleasure and amusement. 'I like Geoff Forrest,' he said. 'I shouldn't think there's much that escapes him.'

The moment he had made this remark he regretted it because he knew that Brenda's feelings about it would be so very different from his own. 'Talking about getting married,' he went on hurriedly before Brenda had a chance to say anything, 'I had an idea the other night but I don't suppose you want to hear about it at the moment.'

'I ought to be going in a minute,' said Brenda, not particularly encouragingly but not particularly repressively either.

Laurie hurried on. It wasn't really the right moment to put forward his suggestion, but at least they were being reasonably friendly to each other, and it might be a long time before even such a suitable moment as this arose again.

'I know you don't want us to marry until we've got a

regular income and I've finished being a student,' he said, 'and basically I agree with you. But I've been thinking about it a lot, and I don't see why we shouldn't do it the other way round. I mean I'm getting a bit sick of being a student and I'd like to start earning a living now and do my D.Phil. later on when I've had some experience of life, as they say. I'd come much more fresh to it then.'

He faltered slightly over this outrageous lie, but struggled gamely on.

'They won't take me in the state system without any training in teaching but there are plenty of independent schools who are willing to give people jobs on the strength of an Oxford history first alone. And universities too. Honestly, darling, I'm sure I could get a reasonable job straight away and I'd be earning enough for you not to have to go to work in stinky caffs and you could hang on and wait until you got the sort of work you really want to do. And I could take up the research later on or do it part-time perhaps. I'll ask TT about it.'

He finished in a rush and then drew in a quick breath. He was a very honest boy and it did not come easily to him to put on this particular act. He had the love and the heroism to suggest making what was for him a very great sacrifice, giving up at least for the time being his own darling project that was to win him even higher academic honours, but he had not the skill and experience to make it appear as if it were not a sacrifice at all. He had got up as he was speaking and Brenda had stood up too. They faced each other now, standing right in the centre of the carpet of the sitting-room of their first home together, Laurie's angular face flushed, unhappy, hopeful and despairing all at the same time, and Brenda with a strange inscrutable expression on her face, a timeless expression that made her look no longer young but not old either, an expression that seemed to hold in it something of both the wisdom and the resignation of women at all ages of history.

At last she smiled faintly and said: 'If there's any sacrificing of careers to be done, I'm the one who's going to do it. I've got nothing much ahead of me really. You've got plenty. You know, Laurie, I think I could be a burden to you. I think you could find a girl who would suit you much better than I do.'

'Brenda!' It came out as a sort of cry and sob combined. 'Don't. Please don't talk like that. I can't bear it.'

'I'm sorry.' She put her arms round him and he laid his head on her shoulder. 'We won't talk any more now. It's not the right moment. Let's wait till things have calmed down here a bit. I've got a job to do and you ought to be getting on with your reading. I'll have to go now. But, Laurie . . .'

She had let him go and now came back to hold him once again.

'Thank you for suggesting it,' she whispered, and then finally tore herself away and ran out of the room.

He had the impression that she was about to burst into tears. Indeed he felt not far off them himself. It seemed to him that the gulf between them was wider than ever, that like Orpheus and his Eurydice, they were dwelling in different worlds.

CHAPTER XII

ABOUT HALF AN HOUR later Terence Toogood came up the attic stairs and knocked on the door of the flat. Laurie opened it and said, 'Oh, hullo. Come in,' in an absent-minded and not particularly welcoming voice. Ever since Brenda had gone downstairs again he had been sitting staring gloomily at the hearthrug, pondering over her last few sentences and trying to decide whether they were intended as a hint that he was about to be given the push.

Terence followed him into the living-room and sat down in the chair where Brenda usually sat.

'Having paid my respects in the drawing-room,' he said, 'I feel entitled to a little relaxation in the more Bohemian part of the house. How are the liberated ladies coming along?'

This was Terence's customary method of enquiring about Laurie's studies. He had chosen a topic connected with the history of women's education, an unusual choice for a male student. But then Laurie was unusual in many ways. For someone of his age, he had exceptional powers of judgement and of imaginative sympathy, which gave his work a breadth and openness that was seldom met with in a youngster. Terence admired him greatly and had high hopes for him. In twenty or thirty years' time, when he himself was a very old man and Laurence Kingston a very famous middle-aged one, it would give him great satisfaction to be able to tell everybody that Laurence had been his discovery, his protégé. Just as he himself had been Professor Francis

Merriman's. With the great difference, of course, that although he himself had acquired a tolerable reputation as a scholar, he never had been and never would be in the very front rank. But Laurie was, and would remain there.

Not only that, but he was something even rarer still: a front-ranker who also happened to be a remarkably sane and well-balanced young man, and not an obvious candidate for a mental hospital as so many of the brainiest ones were. And he had acquired that balance and sanity in the teeth of all the prognostications of sociological theorists, who would no doubt class him as a disadvantaged child in nearly every respect – alcoholic mother, ineffectual father making the worst of a bad situation, one brother on probation for vandalism and another going the same way – that was Laurie's home background. Most youngsters with rotten homes either traded on them and made them an excuse for all their own shortcomings or else they turned their backs on them completely and cut themselves off from their childhood.

Laurie did neither. He seemed to have come to terms with his own roots and had risen splendidly above the poor soil from which he had sprung – a tough sturdy wild plant flourishing on a dung-heap, soaking up the air and the sunlight and the rain, reminding all those who saw it of the wonders that nature could perform and giving them both hope and joy.

That was Terence Toogood's opinion of Laurie, and he was very shocked now to see how strained and unhappy the boy looked.

'I've not had much time to read yet this vacation,' said Laurie. Then he added, with an attempt at a laugh: 'But I've got enough material for a thesis on tourists' reactions to Oxford.'

'Somewhat limited in variety, I imagine,' said Terence.

'Very limited. They all fall into two main categories. The first one is, "Aren't these old buildings romantic?" and the second one is, "My feet are killing me".'

Terence gave his characteristic chuckle, which was rather like a short series of little snorts, before he spoke again. 'Oxford in long vacation. Quite frightful. It always was, even in my own youth. Seriously, Laurence, I do hope you are not wearing yourself out with these unrewarding audiences. You know that in cases of financial difficulties there are always ways and means.'

He stopped rather abruptly. He was not often at a loss for words, but to offer money to Laurie was a very delicate operation. If the boy had a fault, it was a touchy independence about such matters. One had to proceed with tact and subtlety. Arranging for Laurie and his girl to have this nice flat cheap had been an instance of Terence's tactful attempts to help. Unfortunately it did not seem to be turning out very satisfactorily. In fact that was an understatement. From what he had seen and heard downstairs in the big drawing-room over an after-dinner cup of coffee this evening, Terence Toogood had come to the conclusion that Beechcroft was no place for an outstanding student to pursue his studies, nor indeed for any student of any kind.

It could not be said that the scales had completely fallen from his eyes, but he had gained a considerable insight into the tensions and passions that were playing havoc with this apparently well-ordered household, and he blamed himself bitterly for having been so blind to them up till now. He had come upstairs with the intention of getting Laurie right out of it as quickly as possible, but this was easier to resolve upon than to execute. Perhaps the best thing to do was to go straight to the point. The type of subtle diplomacy that he would employ with colleagues of his own generation would not work at all with Laurie.

'I'd very much like to help you if I possibly can,' he said. 'For my own satisfaction even more than for yours. I'm feeling very guilty towards you. I did you a great disservice in bringing you here, although in self-justification I must say that I had no idea at the time how matters lay.'

'It's a very nice flat,' said Laurie formally. 'It was very kind of you to think of us.'

'Oh my dear boy!' cried Terence with unaccustomed warmth. 'Please don't heap coals of fire on my head! If you want to do anything for me, then let me remedy my error. Come and stay at my place for a few weeks and keep me company through the dead month of August. Mrs Harkness will be there to do for us and to act as chaperone to two men who might be open to suspicion if they were alone in the house. To such a pass have we come in our sex-obsessed society! You can have all the books you want and I certainly shall not interfere with your reading, although I shall be there if you want any advice that I am capable of giving. And you will be only a few minutes away from Beechcroft so you can pop round to see Brenda at any time. Please consider it, Laurence. I do most earnestly beg you. You must get out of this house. And quickly. It is not healthy for you. Indeed it isn't.'

Terence was leaning forward with his hands clasped together almost as if in supplication. He was speaking with great feeling and the eyes behind the steel-rimmed spectacles were full of concern and even distress. Laurie had never known his tutor so deeply affected by anything.

In fact he felt very moved himself. After all the emotional ups and downs of the last few days and the sense of hovering on the edge of an abyss that Brenda's remark about his being too good for her had left him with, this kind and generous offer from a man whose integrity was surely beyond all question came as a light in the gloom, a firm foothold in the morass. To live in that peaceful and comfortable household and to have the run of TT's books was an attractive prospect indeed. It was not pride that was leading him to turn down the offer, because he could see that the older man's state of mind was such that it really would be doing him a kindness to accept it.

Laurie said this aloud. 'It's not just my prickly independence, honestly, TT,' he said. 'I can't tell you how much I'd like to come. It sounds like heaven. But I've got to stay here in case something happens that I might have been able to prevent. You do understand, don't you?'

It was his turn to lean forward in a beseeching manner. Terence put an elbow on the arm of his chair, rested his chin on his hand, and stared at the floor. For a full minute neither of them spoke. Then Terence said: 'I know I have the reputation of being something of a gossip, but that only applies to trivial matters. In the case of a really serious situation such as I believe to have arisen in this household, I assure you that I do not gossip. In fact I would much prefer not to talk about it at all, but I fear we can scarcely avoid it entirely. Perhaps if we do talk a little I may be more successful in persuading you to come and stay with me. There's nothing you can do here, you know, Laurence. Those three women downstairs will go their own ways whether you are here or not. You might just as well leave them to get on with it.'

Laurie made no comment.

'I always knew Patience was a pretty slick operator,' continued Terence thoughtfully. 'She made plenty of enemies in the old days when she was holding court in her salon and she'd have made even more if Francis hadn't had the nature of a saint. But she seemed to me to have mellowed greatly with the years, and with her increasing physical infirmity I have recently found her to be more an object of pity than of fear. I confess that I had not realized how much this was the view of an outsider, of one who is content to see only what is on the surface. Because she is no longer a force in Oxford society, I believed her powers to have waned. But I was mistaken. They have come to be concentrated entirely on the domestic front, and in that sphere the claws are as sharp as ever. I am ashamed of myself for being so easily hoodwinked. This evening's conversation was something of a revelation to me.'

After his initial feeling of relief as Terence began to talk, Laurie found himself growing more and more impatient with this delicate skating round the subject.

'What have they been saying?' he burst out. 'Did they talk about Mrs Merriman pretending that Romola had run the car at her this afternoon?'

Terence winced visibly at this crudeness but quickly recovered himself. 'I heard all about it,' he said.

'Who from? Whose version?'

'All three versions. All three ladies found the opportunity to have a quiet word with me, as if it were of supreme importance that I should be persuaded to their view of the affair. I felt rather like a judge being buttonholed by a succession of witnesses.'

'Whom did you believe?' asked Laurie.

'Brenda is obviously speaking what she believes to be the truth,' said Terence. 'She came part of the way upstairs with me just now in order to impress upon me what she had heard and seen. I gather you have heard her story.'

Laurie merely nodded.

'But not either of the others, so whatever conclusions you have drawn must be largely a matter of speculation.'

'Don't you think that Mrs Merriman deliberately ran her chair out in front of the car?' demanded Laurie.

'H'm.' Terence Toogood stroked his chin. 'It's not impossible. That's what Romola said, by the way, when Brenda was taking the old lady along to the cloakroom and we had the opportunity of a few minutes' conversation by ourselves. I think I ought to tell you, Laurence, to save any possible embarrassment, that while I have always had the highest respect for Romola Merriman's character and intelligence, that is as far as my opinion of her goes. She is a woman with whom it is always a pleasure to converse. She is also a woman of great potentialities, so far unrealized. Up till today I was of the opinion that this was by her own free choice. That she should choose to devote herself to her mother rather than spread her own wings was sad but scarcely to be condemned. There are plenty of women even in this selfish society of ours who do exactly the same thing. Gifted women, and intelligent women. Women of fine character and great promise. Who is to say that they should not have sacrificed themselves in this manner? They are full moral agents. They have the choice.'

'Romola Merriman had no choice!' cried Laurie. 'She was bullied and blackmailed into it.'

'Forgive me, Laurence, but I really do not think you

are in a position to judge. I don't think you can possibly
know enough of the facts. Neither, for that matter, do I,
although I have known the family for the best part of
forty years. Known them intimately, I would have said,
but this evening shows me how wrong I should have been
to make that claim.'

Laurie's indignation subsided in the face of this mild
reproof. 'Of course I don't know anything about Romola
Merriman's life,' he admitted. 'I can only guess. But I do
know that her mother is a vicious and evil old woman
who is only out to cause as much destruction and misery
as she possibly can and she's doing her best to break up
Brenda and me. And succeeding,' he added wretchedly.

'No, no. She can't succeed there. Not so long as you
realize what she is trying to do.'

'I realize all right, but Brenda doesn't.'

'I shouldn't be quite so sure about that,' said Terence
thoughtfully. 'Your Brenda is no fool. Has it not occurred
to you that she may be quite right and that the old lady
may indeed be in danger from her own daughter?'

Laurie was obliged to confess that it had.

'Then can you blame Brenda for the way she is acting?'

'I suppose not,' said Laurie grudgingly.

'She has got herself into an extremely difficult position,'
said Terence, 'through no fault of her own but entirely
through her own good qualities. She's taken on a job and
is determined to see it through. How much longer she
can go on protecting and pacifying the old lady without
having an open breach with Romola I really don't know.
The way things look at the moment, I should say that
something has got to give, as they say. But it certainly is
not making it any easier for Brenda to know that you are
skulking miserably up here, with her not daring to come

up to console you. It would be a great deal easier for her if you would come and stay with me. She said so to me herself just now.'

It was this last sentence that tipped Laurie back again. His mind had been acknowledging that Terence's was a powerful argument, and to have Brenda's point of view put clearly to him like that had really caused him to waver. But the knowledge that Terence and Brenda had actually spoken to each other about him filled him with distrust. Suppose after all that TT was no true friend to him but a devil's advocate? Or suppose, more charitably, that Terence's intentions were excellent but that he was in fact doing exactly what Mrs Merriman wanted him to do: get Laurie out of the house?

Laurie spoke all these thoughts aloud, adding that his own deep instinct was to remain at Beechcroft at all costs.

'I thought you were going to say that,' said Terence resignedly and without taking any offence, 'and I can see your point. It's enough to give anybody paranoia, living in this household at the moment with all the intrigue and counter-intrigue that is going on. Patience Merriman's web – that's what we used to call it in her great days. To think she's still spinning away – what a woman!' Terence shook his head as if in reluctant admiration. 'Now mind you take care of yourself, young Laurence, and don't add one more to the number of flies caught in that web already. Keep out of it as much as you can. Brenda will help you to keep out, I am sure. Incidentally, whether or not I am playing Patience's game in trying to get you out of the house, I think you ought to know that my conscious motive is a somewhat selfish one. The status of a man in my position depends very much on the quality of his students, and my stock will slump considerably if my best-ever student is going to make a balls-up of his studies because of domestic problems.'

Terence wagged a finger at Laurie.

'Remember that,' he went on, 'and have some thought for me too. And remember that the offer remains open. Also that if you need my help or advice, in whatever capacity and for whatever it is worth, you know my phone number and can ring it any time.'

He stood up. 'I suppose I had better go down and make some valedictory noises in the drawing-room. And there's one more thing to remember,' he said as they moved towards the door. 'As if you needed reminding of it! Should anybody chance to wonder what you and I have been talking about this last half hour, we have of course been having a fascinating discussion on the part played by the dissenting academies in the education of English girls of gentle birth.'

Laurie achieved a faint smile. 'Of course,' he said. 'It was a most absorbing discussion, wasn't it?'

'Very.'

Laurie's smile had faded by the time they got to the door of the flat and he looked both very young and very worried. 'I say, TT,' he began.

'Laurence?'

'Do you really think Romola Merriman might kill her mother?'

'I wouldn't blame her if she did,' was the not very reassuring reply. 'The wonder is that nobody has done it before. Speaking for myself, I've many a time felt like murdering Patience. Not of recent years, but the feeling is beginning to return tonight. What method should one adopt? A crippled old lady ought not to be too difficult to dispose of. Poisoning would appear to be out, in view of her watchdog. Perhaps a good old-fashioned blow with a blunt instrument would be quickest and most reliable.'

Laurie tried to laugh, as no doubt he was intended to, but found it very difficult. These words presumably spoken in jest were hitting uncomfortably near the mark as far as he himself was concerned.

CHAPTER XIII

'IF YOU WOULD leave my chair just here,' said Mrs Merriman to Brenda, 'at the other side of the bed, then I can get to it easily when I need to transport myself to the lavatory during the night.'

Brenda did as she was told. The wheels ran smoothly and silently across the carpet. It always surprised her how light and easily manoeuvred the chair was. Like those of the half-paralysed athletes you sometimes saw on the television screen, whizzing around with incredible speed and agility and playing ball games. Mrs Merriman managed to whizz around pretty freely too, and the chair had not suffered at all during the afternoon's incident in the front garden of Beechcroft.

The same could hardly be said of the chair's owner. She lay against the pillows in her pink nightgown but her hair seemed to have lost its gloss and the lines in the face were more noticeable than the delicacy of the complexion. She still looked a pathetic and frightened old lady but no longer a surprisingly pretty one.

'Won't you ring for me if you need to get out?' said Brenda. 'You've got your bell here.' And she touched the little brass bell that stood on the bedside table.

'I don't want to rouse the whole house,' said Mrs Merriman quite pettishly. 'It sounds like a clarion call in the dead of night.'

'Oh dear.' Brenda thought for a moment. 'Perhaps it would be better if I slept in here with you.'

She looked around her. It was quite a big room, but scarcely big enough to take the wide settee in the drawing-room on which she was now sleeping.

'Perhaps I could push two chairs together,' she said doubtfully.

'Nonsense.' Mrs Merriman was suddenly brisk. 'You need your sleep. You're looking very tired and I won't hear of such a thing. I can manage.'

'There's the commode,' said Brenda.

'I am not going to use that thing,' said Mrs Merriman. 'When the day comes that I have to depend upon other people to perform disagreeable offices for me, I should much prefer to be dead.'

'But I don't mind emptying it a bit!' cried Brenda. 'I like looking after you. You know I do.'

'Yes, my dear child, I really believe you do.'

Mrs Merriman's hand, swollen and knotted but with some strength in it still, reached out for the firm square hand of the girl standing by the bed. 'It's about the only thing I do believe,' she added, with a quick change back to weakness and pathos. 'Apart from you, I don't trust anybody. Anybody at all.'

'You're worn out,' said Brenda, 'and you need some sleep. I'm sure those new tablets that Dr Forrest left you will help you to rest. I'll go and make the Ovaltine now. I won't be long.'

But Mrs Merriman clung to Brenda's hand and looked up at her with very frightened eyes.

'Where is she?' she asked in a whisper.

'Romola has gone up to bed,' said Brenda soothingly. 'I'm sure she won't be down again tonight.'

Mrs Merriman subsided, looking only partially re-assured, and by the time Brenda got back from the kitchen she had worked herself up into a state of great agitation.

'I brought a cup for myself too,' said Brenda, 'and I'll drink it with you and sit by you till you fall asleep. I'm sure you'll go off quickly with these new tablets. Dr Forrest said you could take two if necessary, but I think it's a good idea to start with just the one, don't you, and have another during the night if you wake up.'

She shook a couple of little white tablets out on to the palm of her hand. 'I'll leave the extra one so that you can reach it,' she said, 'but I'll put the bottle back on the dressing-table out of the way.'

What she really meant was, where you can't easily get hold of it and swallow too many. Dr Forrest had told her that if she was going to make herself responsible for Mrs Merriman's medicine, this was what she ought to do. He had been extremely tactful and helpful and had not asked too many awkward questions when he had come out of the bedroom after having had a long talk with Mrs Merriman.

'Where is Miss Merriman?' he had asked.

'She went upstairs,' Brenda had replied. 'I don't think she was feeling very well.'

'It must have been a considerable shock to her too,' the doctor said. 'I'll go up and see her in a minute. Meanwhile I gather you are helping out here, Brenda. Some light domestic duties in lieu of rent.'

'Yes, that's what we arranged,' Brenda had said,

relieved that she did not have to explain the situation in full herself.

'It's not a bad idea for students who are willing to take on the extra burden and are quite confident that they can carry it,' said Dr Forrest, thus taking the tension and emotion out of the situation at Beechcroft and making it seem quite normal after all, 'though it has its dangers on both sides, for landladies and students alike. On the whole I would advise students to keep to babysitting several evenings a week or perhaps a little cleaning and shopping. But to take full charge of an elderly invalid is quite an undertaking. However – ' and he had smiled at Brenda – 'from what I remember of you when you brought that attempted suicide to the clinic, you are a young lady of resolution. I'm sure you will be able to manage. But we won't let it go on too long. If both Mrs Merriman and her daughter feel the time has come for a resident domestic and nursing help, then we will make other arrangements. This is no reflection on you, my dear child, but I do not think it right that you should carry this sort of burden for too long. And it isn't fair on your young man either.'

Dr Geoffrey Forrest had stood there in the drawing-room, tall and elegant, as Laurie had later said, and Brenda had felt within her a great surge of relief at the presence of so much adult authority and adult expertise in this alarming household. It was Dr Forrest's remarks that had led to her attempt at reconciliation with Laurie, for that was how she saw their conversation, and it had seemed to be going very well until Laurie suddenly burst out with this crazy idea about giving up his higher degree work and taking some stupid job so that they could get married and Brenda would not have to work. It had upset her so much that she had not been able to cope with it, what with all the other strains and tensions. And she had said something silly that might have upset him. And then Terence Toogood had mentioned his plan for getting Laurie out of the house, and Brenda had thought that an excellent idea and had told Terence so. She was sure she could cope much better if Laurie were safely out of the way and it wouldn't last much longer now that Dr Forrest had got the situation in hand. He knew the Merrimans well; he could manage them and he would sort it all out. It was simply a question of being patient and hanging on until he did so. Surely Laurie must see that?

Brenda had quite forgotten, in the midst of all her preoccupations, that she had not told Laurie that Dr Forrest was going to deal with the situation at Beechcroft.

Brenda's own comforting reflections were, however, to be rudely shaken when she held out to Mrs Merriman the sleeping drug that the doctor had prescribed for her.

Mrs Merriman did not pick up the tablet that lay in the palm of the girl's hand. She stared at it with a frightened expression on her face and shrank back into herself. 'I don't trust that doctor,' she muttered. 'I'm sure Romola has got hold of him and spun him a story. Why did he spend so long upstairs with her after he'd been to see me this afternoon?'

Brenda's heart sank, but she tried to keep her voice patient and steady. 'Romola wasn't feeling well,' she said. 'I think it was the shock. And she did say this morning too that her migraine was very bad again.'

'I don't believe it,' quavered Mrs Merriman. 'She only has migraine to spite me. She was perfectly all right this evening when Terence Toogood was here. Wasn't she?'

'She looked as if she'd got a headache,' said Brenda.

'As well she might have, after what she'd done to me this afternoon!' burst out the old lady, and she began to tremble violently, which was something that she could do more or less at will if the circumstances seemed to require it, but sometimes it rather got out of her control. This was the first time she had performed this particular act for Brenda's benefit, and the girl found it alarming.

'Don't you think you'd better take your tablet, Mrs Merriman?' she said. 'I'm sure it will make you feel better and you'll soon go to sleep. Look – I'll hold the cup for you to drink. It's not a very big tablet. You'll soon swallow it down.'

'No, no!' cried Mrs Merriman, shrinking back into the pillows and continuing to tremble. 'I daren't take anything that man prescribes. He's in league with Romola against me. I know he is.'

Brenda's sigh of despair was audible, but she tried once more.

'He couldn't give you anything that was bad for you, Mrs Merriman,' she said, attempting reasoned argument this time. 'He wouldn't dare. Doctors have to be very careful. If he gave you anything he ought not to, it would be traced back to him at once. Wouldn't it now?'

'Not if he examined my dead body and signed the death certificate,' said Mrs Merriman.

Brenda was momentarily at a loss. She had a feeling that there must be some way to counter this argument but she did not personally know enough about the procedure in cases of sudden death to be able to do so. Mrs Merriman pressed home her advantage.

'Would you trust him?' she said. 'Would you take any medicine that he prescribed?'

'Of course I would!' cried Brenda warmly.

'Then you take one of these tablets too,' said Mrs Merriman. 'That'll make me feel better about it. If we're going to die we'll both die together.' She tried a little laugh, but the effect was ghastly, because both her body and her voice were still shaking almost incessantly.

'If I take a sleeping pill,' objected Brenda, 'then I might sleep so soundly that I shouldn't hear you if you needed me.'

'Don't worry about that,' said Mrs Merriman. 'I'm sure you'll wake up if need be. But I hope you won't. You're looking so worn out, my dear, that you need a good night's sleep. Please take the tablet, Brenda. Please humour a silly old woman's fears. It would make me feel so much better.'

'All right,' said Brenda, since there seemed to be nothing else to say. The prospect of a good night's sleep was indeed enormously attractive, and surely nobody could blame her for giving way in the circumstances. Somehow or other Mrs Merriman must be persuaded to take something to calm her down and if this was the only way . . .

'Thank you. Thank you very much,' said Mrs Merriman, taking the tablet from Brenda's hand at last. 'You're a dear girl and I love you very much. I'll drink my Ovaltine now.'

Brenda turned to fetch the two cups from the dressing-table. She put them on the bedside table, picked up the spare tablet, put it in her mouth, and swallowed it down with a sip of Ovaltine. 'There you are,' she said with a faint smile. 'I'm your food taster. You'll be all right now. Where's your tablet gone?'

'I've swallowed it,' said Mrs Merriman. 'I managed to get it down without any liquid. Wasn't that clever of me?'

Brenda was relieved to see that the old lady was beginning to look a little calmer, but she sat by the bed until it appeared as if Mrs Merriman had gone to sleep. It was a very great effort to keep herself upright, because the drug was obviously both quick-acting and potent. Eventually she got up and staggered across the hall in a daze and fell on to the settee without bothering to take off her dressing-gown and within seconds she was dead to the world.

Mrs Merriman, who was finding the strain of pretending to be asleep almost more than she could cope with, stirred as soon as she heard the faint sound of Brenda leaving the room, and stretched herself. Then she twisted round and put her legs to the floor, reached for her stick and pulled herself upright, and then, awkwardly and painfully, but still moving with a speed that would have amazed even Dr Forrest who believed he knew exactly the true extent of Mrs Merriman's disablement, she got across to the dressing-table where an array of medicine bottles stood, and examined the contents of each one in turn. When she came to a small bottle of tiny white tablets labelled 'To be taken only in emergency – do not exceed the stated dose', she nodded and said to herself: That'll do. That ought to have some effect, particularly if it chances to be taken along with one of the other kind as well. Digitalis or some such thing like that, I believe. Foxglove poison we used to call it when we were young.

Then she struggled into her dressing-gown, slipped the little bottle into its pocket, and moved rather more slowly back to the bed, where she rested for a while, summoning up all her reserves of strength and deciding in what manner she should next proceed. She must not forget, among other things, to get rid of the tablet that she had hidden under the pillow while Brenda's back was turned. It could be flushed down the lavatory or even down the kitchen sink. Or no – wait a moment. It looked very like the other white tablets. Why not drop it in too? Then there was the question of whether or not to wear gloves. It would make her hands even more awkward than they were in any case, but it might nevertheless be a good idea.

Altogether there was a great deal to decide and great risks to be taken, but it was worth it. What was the use of having even one last kick of life left in you if you couldn't rise to a great challenge? It was a very long time indeed since Mrs Merriman had experienced such heights of excited anticipation.

CHAPTER XIV

LAURIE FOUND IT IMPOSSIBLE to get to sleep.

The state of lethargic depression into which he had sunk after Brenda's departure had been converted by Terence's visit into a state of agitated depression instead. He tried to take comfort from the thought of Terence's kindness and high opinion of him, but all that happened was that he acquired a feeling of guilt, in addition to everything else, because he could not feel more grateful to Terence.

He tried reading, writing, listening to music, playing chess with himself, drinking tea, eating apples – everything he could possibly think of to try to quiet his mind, but all without success. If there had been any alcohol in the flat he would have swallowed the lot, but there wasn't any there at the moment. Nothing but some aspirin which he had already tried without any effect and some cough lozenges with a peculiarly revolting flavour that he did not propose to try.

Whatever he did always ended up with his moving restlessly and aimlessly round and round the flat because it was quite impossible to stay still, and thinking that to murder old Mrs Merriman would really be to perform a public service. The thought of murdering Mrs Merriman was the only thought that brought him any relief at all.

At about half past one, when his wanderings had taken him into the bathroom at the back, Laurie moved towards the tiny dormer window cut into the roof of Beechcroft with the vague intention of seeing whether it had started to rain again. It didn't really interest him in the least whether or not it was raining at this hour of the night, but it was something to occupy his mind for a moment or two.

It was not raining, but as he looked down the slope of slates beneath the window to the dimness beyond, in which could just be made out the shapes of trees in the back garden and houses in the next road, he became aware of a sudden change in the view. Where he had been able to see only very dimly, he could now see quite clearly: part of the back lawn, the climbing roses shielding the vegetable garden, the line of runner-beans and various other plants. They all showed up as if in bright moonlight.

But there was no moon. And in any case, the moon didn't suddenly switch itself on like that. Even if it came out from behind a cloud, it didn't have quite that sudden effect. It was a puzzling phenomenon to Laurie's weary mind, and for a moment it fully occupied his thoughts, driving out all the reflections that had been so plaguing him.

When it dawned on him what must be the cause of this change of vision he banged at his forehead and called himself a fool. Of course. Somebody had switched on a light in one of the rooms at the back of the house, and it was that that was lighting up the garden. Which room could it be? Not the attic bathroom in which he was standing, because he had had its light on all the time and in any case the slope of the roof prevented its light from shining on to the lawn. It was unlikely to be any of the first-floor rooms either, because Romola's bedroom was at the front of the house and the two bedrooms at the back were unoccupied. Nor did he think it was Romola going to the bathroom, because that would be too small a window to throw all this light.

No. It could only be coming from one place, and that was the kitchen, which had a big window looking out on to the back garden, and it rather looked as if the curtains had not been drawn across.

So somebody had come into the big kitchen on the ground floor of Beechcroft in the middle of the night and had switched on the light there, and Laurie was attacked by an overwhelming desire to find out who this somebody was. No doubt it would be either Romola or Brenda making tea because they were unable to sleep, and equally certainly neither of them would be particularly pleased to see him, but at least it would give him something to do, a motive for getting through the next few minutes, if he went down to investigate. But it would be best not to switch on the staircase lights. He had an old bicycle lamp whose battery was still functioning, and he could use that if he couldn't manage to make his way down in the dark without bumping into things.

By the time Laurie had come to this decision and found the bike lamp it was about ten minutes since he had first seen the kitchen light showing up the garden. He came slowly and silently down the attic stairs and lingered for a moment outside the door of Romola's bedroom on the first floor. It was shut, but that could mean anything. Feeling rather ashamed of himself and wondering whatever excuse he could make if Romola herself suddenly appeared either from inside or outside the room, Laurie put his ear to the keyhole and listened.

In the dead quiet of the house at this hour of the night he was sure that he could hear the sound of breathing. Or rather, not exactly breathing, but the little noises half-moaning, half-snoring, made by a restless or troubled sleeper.

He straightened up again, ready to swear that Romola was now asleep in her room and had been so for some time. So it must be Brenda in the kitchen. Unless perhaps Mrs Merriman was in there with her. Or unless it was burglars.

This last thought, ridiculous though it seemed, held just enough plausibility to make Laurie hurry on his way. The big staircase was easy enough to negotiate without help from the bicycle lamp because the door of Mrs Merriman's bedroom was ajar and a faint beam of light came into the hall. Laurie's bare feet made no sound on the thick staircarpet, and he moved with great caution. Presumably the old woman left the lamp burning all night and the door open so that she could call for Brenda.

Laurie had reached the bottom of the main staircase when there came to him the feeling that somebody else was in the hall. He was not conscious of having heard anything, and in the area lit by the beam from the bedroom there was nobody to be seen, but the sense of a human presence was very strong within him. He stood on the lowest step for what seemed a very long time, making no sound and no movement, and the other person in the hall did exactly the same.

Then the light came on with such unexpected suddenness that Laurie blinked and shivered and became momentarily paralysed, like some wild creature strayed on to a road and caught in the glare of a car's headlights. When the first shock was over he had an unpleasant sensation of being completely defenceless and naked, although in fact he was perfectly respectably clothed in his pyjamas. All sorts of images and impressions flashed through his mind, mostly drawn from films and books and television programmes, and all unpleasant. To have your protective cloak of silent darkness suddenly ripped off you was a nasty experience at any time, even if the light did not suddenly confront you with a man pointing a gun at your head.

But even that, thought Laurie, would have felt less menacing to him than what he actually did see, which was an old woman dressed in a pink quilted dressing-gown and sitting in a wheelchair. Hardly a terrifying prospect in itself, but the look on that old woman's face at this moment made Laurie's blood run cold. He had never before seen such concentrated malevolence on any human face: he would not have believed it possible.

'Well?' she said, moving the chair from where it stood just outside the door of the drawing-room and coming towards him at such speed that he instinctively stepped back on to the safety of the bottom stair. 'Well? Do you wish to explain yourself?'

'I thought I heard burglars,' said Laurie.

It sounded both very feeble and very absurd, but he could not think of anything else to say, and there was just a faint element of truth in it.

'Burglars!' Mrs Merriman gave a little laugh, not very loud but extraordinarily sinister and disagreeable. 'Burglars!'

'But now I can see that everything's all right,' said Laurie retreating still further up the stairs, 'I'll go back to bed.'

'Yes. You do that,' said Mrs Merriman, positioning her chair across the bottom of the stairs and turning her head to look up at him with malicious glee. 'You go back to bed.' And the little laugh came again.

Laurie turned and ran hastily upstairs, not pausing until he reached the attic staircase, well out of sight of anyone in the hall. For a moment or two he had the impression that she was going to get out of her chair and hobble or crawl up the stairs after him and the thought of this was indescribably horrible. He told himself that it was utterly ridiculous for a strong and healthy young man to be running in terror from a crippled old woman but it didn't make any difference to his feelings. It was no use his reason telling him that she could not possibly do him any harm. The thing was beyond reason. It's like the fear of witches, said Laurie to himself, and indeed the overwhelming sense of evil and malevolence that he had felt in Mrs Merriman's presence was like some super-human fear.

She's put a spell on me, he said to himself as he retreated to the flat at the top: I don't think I'll have the courage to go down again, although I do want to see if

Brenda is all right.

This sense of menace took some time to die down. Laurie sat on his bed with his chin on his hands, struggling to regain his balance and his common sense, but whenever there came one of those faint creaking sounds that are always to be heard in any house at dead of night, he felt the apprehension rising again, and saw in his imagination a revolting sight of a bent and crippled old woman crawling slowly up the stairs like some monstrous lumbering insect, coming nearer and nearer, bearing within it some force against which human strength and human reason would struggle in vain.

You've been watching too many science fiction programmes, said Laurie to himself, and eventually he managed to shake the feeling off and to think rationally about Mrs Merriman's presence in the front hall of Beechcroft at this hour of the night and about the little incident that had driven him to go downstairs in the first place, the light shining over the back garden from the kitchen on the ground floor. Laurie was glad that he had not mentioned this light to Mrs Merriman, because it must have been she who was in the kitchen. Had it been Brenda he would have seen or heard some sign of her.

No. It had been Mrs Merriman on her own, and she had got as far back to her room as the opposite side of the hall when she had become aware of Laurie on the staircase, for that she had known of his presence before he knew of hers he had no doubt. The old woman had got out of her bed and propelled herself into the kitchen. Of course there could be an innocent explanation for her furtiveness, but Laurie did not think it was in her nature to be very quiet because she did not want to disturb anybody else's sleep. The only reason why she had been creeping around like that was that she was doing something that she didn't want anybody else to know about.

What could it be? Here Laurie's imagination began to fail him. He didn't know enough of the ways of the household downstairs to make a guess. The nearest he could get, taking the incident of the previous afternoon as a guide, was that Mrs Merriman had been doing something in the kitchen to make it seem that Romola was trying to kill her. Putting poison into some food or drink that she alone took, so that she could sniff suspiciously at it the following day and denounce Romola. If that were the case, no wonder she was furious at being caught by Laurie not far from the scene of the act. That would account for the expression on her face.

But it was taking a great risk and it was amazing that Brenda had not heard her. The more Laurie thought about this the more worried he became, and at last he could bear it no longer and decided to go downstairs once more, even at the risk of encountering Mrs Merriman again, in order to assure himself that no harm had come to Brenda. This time all was dark and silent and still. Even the light in Mrs Merriman's bedroom had been turned out. Laurie used the bicycle lamp, carefully blinkering its beam with his hand. It was better to risk being seen rather than to risk another such unnerving encounter.

Nothing happened. He came into the drawing-room without being disturbed and moved quietly to where Brenda lay on the big settee. He shone the bicycle lamp on to her and for a moment or two his heartbeat quickened. Brenda was lying not in her usual womblike position but sprawled precariously near to the edge of the settee, with one arm trailing to the floor. She was wearing her dressing-gown and lying on top of the makeshift bed.

Laurie's heightened and frightened imagination saw her momentarily not as a living girl asleep but as a dead one, lying in a position that would have been unnatural to her in life.

He bent closer and saw that although she appeared to be completely motionless, she was in fact breathing regularly. The relief was very great but his mind was still not quite at ease. Brenda would only look like that for one of three reasons: she was seriously ill or she was drunk or she was drugged. Illness of such severity could be ruled out, and that she was drunk was equally unlikely. Drugged was the answer but the question remained whether it had been willingly or unwillingly and Laurie was almost sure that it was the latter. His rather vague speculations about what had been going on downstairs began to take a more concrete form.

He put his arms round Brenda's limp body and shifted it to the centre of the wide settee. She stirred and moaned a little but did not wake. Then he lifted her wrist to feel the throb of the blood. It was slow but regular and steady. He shone the bicycle lamp on to her again and looked at her closely and ran over in his mind the relevant first-aid classes that he had attended. After thinking it over for a little longer he decided not to telephone the doctor. Whatever drug it was that Brenda had been induced to take was not doing her any harm. If what he now suspected were true, then it was probably no more than a strong sleeping pill and Brenda, unused to narcotics, had reacted strongly.

Well, sleep would not hurt her, thought Laurie, but he was determined not to leave her alone. He bent over and kissed her closed eyes and then shifted her further over until she was right up against the back of the settee, leaving just enough room for him to lie down beside her, which he did.

And so the hours passed till dawn.

CHAPTER XV

'DARLING,' said Brenda sleepily. 'Darling Laurie.'

A minute later she was shaking him vigorously. 'Laurie! Wake up. You can't stay down here.'

Laurie came out of a nightmare of falling off the edge of a cliff and actually did slip from the edge of the settee on to the floor.

'My God, it's half past eight!' cried Brenda. 'I'm supposed to make her tea at half past seven. Hurry up, Laurie, get moving.'

Laurie was still sitting dazedly on the carpet.

'Aren't you going to work?' asked Brenda.

He got up with an effort. 'I suppose so.' Then he grinned at her. 'Aren't you? Hadn't you better go and explain yourself to the boss?'

'Oh shut up! I'm going to get the tea.'

'I think I'll have some too,' he said, following her into the kitchen.

'I do wish you'd get out of my way,' said Brenda, pushing Laurie aside from the sink where he was checking to see whether any pans or crockery had been used during the night.

'What on earth are you doing, Laurie?' she cried a moment later even more impatiently.

Laurie had taken a bottle of bleach out of a cupboard

and was unscrewing the top. It had occurred to him that
Mrs Merriman might have been messing about with the
various household poisons during the night, and if the
bottle tops were loose that could well be because they had
last been handled by fingers without much strength in
them.

The bleach bottle top was screwed on tight, and so
was that containing a very potent oven-cleaner. He glanced
around the kitchen and wondered what to look for next.
Whatever the old woman had been doing would surely be
below shoulder level. Even if she were far more active
than anybody realized, she would hardly be able to
climb on a chair to reach the wall cupboards or shelves.
But that still left an awful lot of places where she could
have set some sort of lethal booby-trap.

'We've got plenty of disinfectant upstairs!' cried
Brenda as Laurie inspected yet another bottle. 'What's
the matter with you? What were you doing down here
last night anyway?'

'I cannot live without my love,' said Laurie, blowing a
kiss at her with a melodramatic gesture. Then he walked
into the little lobby that led from the kitchen to the back
door and groaned inwardly at the sight of so many more
potentialities. There were bottles of fertilizer and weed-
killer here, notorious domestic killers, not to mention a
whole cupboard that would be well within the old woman's
reach. Perhaps it would be better to abandon the poison
end of it and concentrate instead on the food and drink
that Mrs Merriman was likely to take. For at this moment
he was still convinced that Mrs Merriman's nocturnal
activities had the aim of making it appear that she was in
danger from her daughter.

'What's that?' he asked as Brenda took a jug from the

fridge and poured liquid into a small glass.

'Grapefruit juice,' she replied resignedly. Laurie was in one of his clowning moods and there was nothing to be done with him. He picked up the glass from Mrs Merriman's tray and sniffed at it.

'It smells funny,' he said. 'I shouldn't give it to her if I were you, Bren. Can't you open a new tin?'

'What's the matter with it?' Brenda snatched the glass from Laurie's hands. 'Smells all right to me. And tastes all right too.' She took a sip of it and put it back on the tray while Laurie cast his eyes upward and made extravagant gestures of despair. In fact he had not at all liked it when Brenda drank from the glass, but on the other hand it seemed better to go on fooling around like this rather than tell her of his serious suspicions. And surely whatever Mrs Merriman had done could not cause any real harm: it would be intended to look like attempted murder, not actually to bring about a murder.

Or would it? Would it perhaps give her some twisted satisfaction to poison the whole household, herself included? Laurie wished he could feel sure that this was not about to happen.

'Does she have grapefruit juice every morning?' he asked.

'That or orange,' said Brenda.

'What else?'

'Toast and marmalade and tea. Oh Laurie, do go away! You're not being funny. You're just being a nuisance.'

Laurie had picked up the little glass dish containing marmalade and was spooning some of it into his mouth.

'Tastes home-made,' he said. 'Rather good.'

'Have some, then,' snapped Brenda in an exasperated

voice. 'Here you are, infant.' And she took a saucer from the plate-rack and a glass jar from a cupboard and spooned out some of the marmalade.

'Thank you,' said Laurie very seriously as he took it from her hand. 'That's a big enough sample for someone at the science labs to analyse. I'd like to know the ingredients.'

It was as near as he dared go to telling her his suspicions. He was longing to tell her about his encounter with Mrs Merriman in the night, but was afraid that that would bring the barriers right up between Brenda and himself again. Not only that, but he could not get rid of the superstitious feeling that whoever knew about Mrs Merriman's excursion was in some way at risk, and it would be better for Brenda not to know. And it would also be better to stop irritating her now and leave her to get on with it, while he himself went and washed and shaved and dressed before carrying out the next part of his programme, which was to warn Romola.

Ten minutes later he came downstairs again to find the door of Romola's bedroom open. He looked in and saw the bed was unmade and Romola was not there. She did not appear to be in the bathroom either, so presumably she had gone downstairs. Beginning to wish that he had not waited to get dressed before going to talk to her, Laurie took the bottom flight of stairs three at a time and rushed back to the kitchen. There was nobody there and no sign of any breakfast being prepared. He glanced out into the garden, but she was not there either, or at any rate nowhere within view. The next place to look was the drawing-room.

Brenda had folded up the bedclothes and replaced the cushions on the settee, but the room still felt faintly stuffy and occupied and in some way rather disturbing. At first Laurie thought that this big room, too, was empty, and then he saw Romola, sitting in her dressing-gown in the armchair to the right of the fireplace, with the light from the window falling on to her face.

It looked ghastly: haggard and greenish, that of an old woman sick to death. Laurie rushed forward.

'Miss Merriman – Romola – what's wrong? You're ill. I'll get the doctor quick.'

'No.' The lovely voice was faint but clear. 'It's only migraine. I get it very badly. I'll be better soon. I've taken two of my pills. They always work.'

She shut her eyes and sat rigid, her hands gripping the arms of the chair. It looked as if she were in agony. Laurie knew quite a bit about migraine because he had very occasional bad attacks of it himself, and he did not like the look of Romola at all.

'Where are your pills?' he asked, hating to question anybody in such a state of misery but convinced that something needed to be done urgently.

'In the drawer of the kitchen table,' was the reply, the voice even fainter now than previously. 'I don't think I'd better take any more.'

Laurie did not wait to listen to this last sentence. He shot out of the room and into the kitchen and found the little bottle, along with a bottle of vitamin tablets, at the front of the table drawer. He picked it up, glanced at it, saw that there were about a dozen small white tablets inside, and took it with him to the telephone which was in a little alcove under the stairs. At the very moment when he was searching on the pad for the doctor's number, Mrs Merriman was saying petulantly to Brenda: 'No, no. I'm not going to take my heart tablet.

I don't trust that doctor.'

'But you've already had half those in this bottle,' said Brenda, picking it up. 'They've done you no harm so far. So why should the other ones harm you?'

'Don't trust him, don't trust him. And don't trust Romola,' muttered the old woman.

Brenda gave a little shrug and replaced the bottle among the others on the dressing-table. 'Which dress do you want to wear?' she asked.

At the telephone Laurie was dialling Dr Geoffrey Forrest's number. To his enormous relief he was told that the doctor was there, just starting a morning surgery.

'It's terribly urgent,' said Laurie. 'It's Miss Romola Merriman. It looks as if she's been poisoned.'

The female voice put him straight through to Dr Forrest. Evidently the name Merriman worked wonders when it came to getting prompt medical attention. Unless he had been expecting something like this, thought Laurie as he quickly explained.

'Yes, I've got the tablets,' he said in reply to a brief question. 'I'll hold on to them. You'll be coming?'

'Five minutes,' was the reply. 'My partner will see to surgery. Don't do anything. Just stay by her.'

Laurie put down the receiver, turned round, and came face to face with Brenda.

'What on earth is going on?' she asked. 'Mrs Merriman heard someone telephoning. She wants to know what's happened.'

'Then she'll bloody well have to wait!' cried Laurie, taking Brenda by the arms and putting her to one side. 'As if she didn't know already!' he added as he ran back to the drawing-room.

CHAPTER XVI

'SHE'LL BE ALL RIGHT,' said Dr Forrest to Laurie in the waiting-room of the nursing home some hours later. 'It probably would not have been fatal, but it was very nasty and I'm most grateful to you for acting so promptly. It was the combination of the drugs that had such a drastic effect. Most unfortunate that she happened to shake out one of each. A couple of the migraine tablets would have been fine, and a couple of the others wouldn't have done her much harm. But the two mixed together . . .'

He shrugged and left the sentence unfinished.

'Anyway, thank you again. And Miss Merriman has asked me to thank you too, but she doesn't feel up to talking just yet. Better let her sleep it off till tomorrow. She'll be all right here. They charge through the nose but they're reliable.'

'I wish she didn't have to go back to Beechcroft at all,' said Laurie.

The tall man in the grey suit looked at him with interest. 'I think you and I had better have a proper talk now that all the excitement has died down,' he said. 'I can spare another half hour or so. Where shall we go? To my place? Or would you rather I came back with you to Beechcroft to cast my eyes over things there?'

'Please,' said Laurie. 'If you could. I'd rather tell you there. And if you could only get Brenda away . . .'

They reached the doctor's car and were walking up the path to the front door of Beechcroft a few minutes later. Laurie put his key into the lock and Brenda, hearing it, came from the kitchen to greet them.

'How is she?' was her first question.

'Much better.' It was Laurie who replied.

'Thank God,' cried Brenda with the most heartfelt relief.

'Thank Laurence,' said Dr Forrest. 'He's the hero of this particular operation.'

Brenda gave Laurie a look that made his heart rejoice. It's all going to be all right, said that look as plainly as anything. But to Dr Forrest she said: 'What are we going to do about Mrs Merriman? She says she doesn't want to see you any more.'

'Then she need not see me,' was the calm reply. 'She can see my partner if she wishes. If not, she may take her custom elsewhere.'

'I wonder whether I'd better,' began Brenda, and was interrupted by a loud cry from the direction of the drawing-room.

'Brenda! Brenda! Don't let that man come near me. Get him out of this house. Quickly!'

The voice was shrill and very near hysterics. The three standing in the hall stared at each other for a moment. Then Dr Forrest raised his eyebrows, Laurie looked anxiously at Brenda, and Brenda, with a little shrug and a somewhat melodramatic movement of the hands unusual in her, said softly: 'You see? That's how it is.'

'I am here purely as Laurie's guest,' said Dr Forrest loudly, 'and we are going up to the flat straight away.'

He led the way upstairs, with Laurie following, while the cries from the drawing-room became even more demanding and Brenda ran off making despairing gestures and looking even more unlike her usual stolid self.

When they reached the flat at the top Laurie cried excitedly: 'I've remembered it! Incredible that I've not remembered before, but she scared me stiff. That was part of the witch-like impression.'

'What have you remembered?' asked Dr Forrest, seating himself.

'Gloves! She was wearing gloves when I saw her in the wheelchair. Black gloves. It registered and then went away again and it's only just come back. But I'd swear to it anywhere.'

'And she doesn't usually wear gloves in the house. I see,' said Dr Forrest.

'Fingerprints, I suppose,' said Laurie, 'which means that she really did hope for some result when she put some of her own tablets in with Romola's. But she couldn't have known what result, could she?'

'Hardly,' said the doctor, 'since we had some difficulty in identifying and dealing with it ourselves. I should say that it was done with the general aim of causing some sort of mischief rather than with any real hope of poisoning her daughter.'

There was a controlled anger in the voice that made Laurie look at the grey-haired man with interest and with a sudden suspicion. Of course Dr Forrest had been doing his very best to help Romola ever since Laurie's urgent telephone call, but that was his job and any doctor would or should have done the same. And the Merrimans were private patients, no doubt paying good fees, although Laurie hoped that was not too strong a consideration because he liked the doctor very much. It was at this moment, however, that Laurie for the first time suspected Geoffrey of an interest that went beyond the purely professional.

'Why does Mrs Merriman hate her daughter so much?' he asked, with some hope of satisfying his own curiosity.

'Because she is a daughter and not a son,' was the reply. 'Mrs Merriman is one of those women whose own frustrated ambitions have found an outlet through another person. She has a first-class mind, but in her youth and with her social background this was not considered an asset for a woman. Instead of putting it to direct constructive use, she used it in a twisted way first of all to further her husband's career and then to frustrate her daughter's.'

'But if she was frustrated in her own ambition,' began Laurie slowly.

'Yes, one might think she would have been all the keener for her daughter to have a chance,' concluded Dr Forrest for him. 'Yes. It can work that way. But she is not a very nice person. Normal human affection, particularly maternal affection, is quite lacking. With sons she would have continued as she did with her husband, pushing them on, being the power behind the throne, never letting them see her real self. They'd have worshipped her. And with a genuinely dull and downtrodden daughter it would not have been quite so bad. She'd have been turned into a household drudge, of course, but a stodgy insensitive woman would not have suffered so very much from that, and there would have been no need to treat her with such mental cruelty. Instead of this, she had a girl of unusual gifts and unusual character and this was the one thing that Mrs Merriman could not endure.'

The doctor spoke very calmly, almost as if relating a clinical case history, but Laurie felt that his question was answered. Here indeed was the one 'friend' at whom

Romola had hinted, and who indeed should know her better than the man who had known the household for years and had seen it at all times, at its very worst and not only with its smooth social surface?

'I wondered whether Romola might have been an actress if she'd had the chance,' he said almost shyly, feeling very humble at this glimpse into a world of adult tragedy that up till now had been outside his own experience.

'An actress? No, not an actress. A singer,' said Dr Forrest. 'An opera singer probably. That's what she wanted to be, and with any other parents that's what she would have been. To do him justice, if her father had been left to himself, she would have been trained. He seems to have had an idea of the girl's talents but her mother managed to convince him that Romola was temperamentally unsuited for such a career. For any career, come to that. Don't let us blame Francis Merriman too much. Patience Merriman is a diabolically clever woman.'

'And what is going to happen now?' asked Laurie.

'I can't tell you,' replied the doctor, 'but I know what is not going to happen. Romola is not coming back to this house so long as her mother is living in it.'

'Cheers!' cried Laurie, raising both hands in the air and clapping them together. 'By the way I never told you, did I, about what Brenda saw when Mrs Merriman asked her to fetch her diary.'

And he proceeded to do so, Dr Forrest listening without interruption and saying nothing but 'Thank you for telling me', when Laurie had finished.

'Oughtn't she to be prosecuted or something, for mixing up the tablets?' ventured Laurie when it looked as if the doctor was not going to speak further.

'You feel you have sufficient evidence that she did this?' was the rather brusque comment on this suggestion.

'Well, somebody did,' said Laurie, 'and I saw her, and she was wearing those black gloves.' It sounded rather lame, even as he spoke, and he was not surprised by Dr Forrest's reaction.

'Would you like to stand up against even a reasonably competent defence counsel in a court of law and produce that as evidence that a poor feeble old woman deliberately tried to make things unpleasant for the daughter who was devoting her life to looking after her mother? Do you think any jury in the country would believe it? Would you believe it yourself, just on the facts?'

Laurie had to admit that he would not.

'And of course you would have to reckon with Patience Merriman herself,' continued the doctor. 'You would find her a very slippery customer indeed. Even if it could be proved that she mixed up the tablets, that does not in itself prove malice. An old lady like that! Who had had a terrible shock earlier in the day when the car nearly ran her down and who was probably still suffering from the after-effects of shock. Of course she got muddled. Old people do get muddled. And she'd had a heavy sedative to help her to sleep. She might have woken and gone in a dazed condition to the kitchen looking for her own tablets and wondered whether they were the right ones after all and then gone back to her room . . . and so on and so forth. If there is any advantage to be gained in pretending to be more or less gaga, then you may be quite sure that is what Patience Merriman will pretend to be. Old people do become senile and confused in mind and no power on earth is going to be able to prove that she knows exactly what she is up to. I shouldn't be at all surprised if she's not paving the way for it now, doing a convincingly muddled act for Brenda's benefit.'

This supposition proved later to be not unfounded. Meanwhile Laurie listened to Dr Forrest with increasing agitation and indignation, and said when he had finished: 'Do you mean that there's nothing at all we can do about her? That she can try to poison Brenda or anyone else who looks after her or even try to poison me and there's nothing we can do to prevent it?'

'I am quite sure she is going to try something else,' said Dr Forrest, 'and if you and Brenda remain here it is up to you to see that she does not succeed.'

'But what can we do?' cried Laurie in despair.

Dr Forrest stood up. 'You know her. You know the sort of thing she gets up to. You'll just have to be on your guard and do your best. You've not been doing so badly so far, Laurence. And you know where I am in case of emergency. Now I've got to go. I've a clinic at four.'

Laurie stood up too, feeling very worried indeed and also disappointed. In spite of all the distress of the last few hours it had been an enormous relief to know that an older person whom he trusted had taken charge and that the responsibility for whatever happened at Beechcroft was not entirely his own. And now this person was clearing off and leaving him to it again. There was Terence to go to, of course, but somehow Laurie didn't quite trust TT in spite of what he had said.

Geoffrey Forrest saw the boy's expression and read it accurately. 'There really is nothing more that I personally can do here,' he said with a faint smile. 'Any influence I may once have had over Patience Merriman is at an end. She has a perfect right to choose her own doctor, and I can't stop her. And you and Brenda are free agents too and go your own ways. What am I to say? Of course you ought to clear out at once, both of you. But are you going to? Of course you aren't. You won't leave Brenda and Brenda won't leave a feeble old woman, vicious though she may be. Isn't that right, Laurence?'

Laurie had to admit that it was. 'But we could go if you'd get in a nurse or a housekeeper to look after her,' he added.

Dr Forrest made a faint sound of impatience. 'My dear boy, do you really suppose Mrs Merriman is going to allow herself to be looked after by any woman suggested by myself?'

'She needn't know it was suggested by you,' retorted Laurie, feeling that this time the doctor's admirable habit of treating young people as young people had gone too far, 'if you'd tell us where to phone.'

'All right. Fair enough.' Dr Forrest pulled out a prescription pad and wrote a couple of addresses and telephone numbers on it. 'Here you are.' He tore off the sheet. 'These are reliable agencies. And I've put the phone numbers where you can get me too.'

Just inside the door of the room he paused to glance at Laurie's chess set that stood on the side table. The board was open and a few pieces were set out in a problem on which Laurie had started during one of his unsuccessful attempts to divert his mind the previous night. The doctor adjusted some of the chessmen and then said: 'There you are. Black queen and two white pawns. White to mate in three moves.'

'The black queen is old and crippled,' said Laurie, 'and as for the other two, pawn is just about the right word. They'll be very lucky if they end up with a draw.'

The doctor laughed and gave him a friendly pat on the shoulder. 'Never mind. That's what life is like. A series of stalemates.'

It's all very well for you, thought Laurie as he followed the older man downstairs: you've got your lady friend safely out of it, which is more than I have.

CHAPTER XVII

THE TRUTH of Dr Forrest's statement was, however, borne out by the commotion to be heard coming from the drawing-room. It burst out as they came to the top of the wide flight of stairs. Mrs Merriman had evidently been waiting to hear the sound of footsteps before she began in earnest.

'Brenda! Brenda!' she screamed. 'Don't let him come near me. Murderer! Deceiver! They've been plotting together, the two of them. Plotting to kill a feeble old woman so that they can get hold of her house and her money.'

And so on in the same vein, fear, pathos and anger nicely blended. Dr Forrest turned to Laurie as they stood in the front hall and raised shoulders and eyebrows in a controlled but eloquent gesture. Laurie replied to the doctor's unspoken comment. 'Oh, all right. I can see you were right and that there is nothing that you can do. Goodbye, Dr Forrest, and thanks for everything.'

Geoffrey Forrest paused for a moment just inside the front door, and then, as if sensing the young man's disappointment and wanting to alleviate it a little, or perhaps in response to some deeply felt urge of his own, he walked straight into the drawing-room and came close to where Mrs Merriman was sitting in her usual place by the window, temporarily exhausted by her histrionic efforts, while Brenda hovered about behind her, looking anxious and miserable.

'Mrs Merriman,' said Dr Forrest very calmly, 'you are talking a lot of rubbish and you know it.'

The old woman jerked her head up and glared at him. 'You – you snake in the grass!' she gasped. 'Making up to my poor daughter behind my back. Money! That's all you're after.' Her eyes brightened and she smiled, not the sweet smile but the deadly one. 'Big houses. Big cars. The best tailors,' she went on. 'Oh yes, I know you, Geoffrey Forrest. You may be a tolerable doctor but you're a very self-indulgent man. And it's not easy to keep it all up, even with the fees you charge, when you've got all that alimony to pay out too. Romola's money would come in very handy. Oh yes, very handy indeed.' Mrs Merriman's head began to shake, but it was with satisfaction, and not with weakness or fear. 'Play your cards right,' she went on, 'and you might even get it without actually having to marry her.'

Laurie had been watching the doctor's face as the old woman was speaking and out of the corner of his eye he could see that Brenda was doing the same. Dr Forrest appeared to be completely unmoved by the attack, but Laurie had the feeling that some of the shots, at least, had gone home. The doctor obviously did take great care over his appearance; he did have a big house and a big car. That he was paying out large sums of money to a former wife was no doubt equally correct.

'Congratulations, Patience,' said Dr Forrest quietly.

'I am glad to see you have abandoned the crude ranting and are back on your old form again. The stock of venom has not yet run out. You have even succeeded in sowing doubts in the minds of our young friends here. Well done. Very well done indeed. You are right in much of what you have said about me. But you are wrong about my feeling for Romola. That is something that is far outside your comprehension, so it is useless to speak of it. I will send you my final account. Would you like to transfer to Dr Sanders, or would you prefer to make other arrangements?'

Mrs Merriman's face still wore its tight little smile. 'I'll transfer to Dr Sanders,' she said. 'A very charming lady. She attended me once when you were on one of your luxury holidays. Yes, a charming girl. No doubt you and she will vastly enjoy yourselves on Romola's money.'

Laurie glanced at Brenda while these last words were being spoken and could tell from her face that she believed their implication. It took a man, it seemed, to appreciate that Romola Merriman could inspire genuine admiration and perhaps even devotion in another man. Brenda's eyes were still only halfway opened: she was still very much caught in the web. Nausea rose in Laurie and he could contain himself no longer. He was just about to burst out and say that it was a bloody slanderous lie, when Dr Forrest forestalled him.

'No doubt we shall,' he said in his most equable way. 'And no doubt you are going to enjoy exercising your powers on Dr Sanders. I will arrange for the transfer.' He made a little bow. 'Goodbye, Mrs Merriman.'

He turned and walked towards the door, smiling and waving at Laurie as he left the room. A moment later the front door closed and there followed the faint hum of a perfect engine in perfect condition and of tyres crunching the gravel.

Mrs Merriman instantly became querulous. 'I'm tired, Brenda. It's all been too much for me. I want to go to bed.'

'All right,' said Brenda, giving Laurie a rather desperate look. 'I'll help you in. Would you like me to get Dr Sanders now?'

'No, no. Not yet. I'm sick of doctors. Scoundrels and scroungers. The whole pack of them.' Her mouth worked and she manoeuvred her chair away from Brenda's outstretched hands and suddenly made it shoot off at great speed towards the spot where Laurie was standing near the door of the big room. He jumped out of the way just in time. Had the front wheels or the foot-rest crashed into his ankles he could have been quite badly bruised and it would certainly have knocked him over. Brenda gave a little gasp. She couldn't say she hadn't seen it this time, thought Laurie with a certain grim satisfaction. Mrs Merriman took no notice of either of them but carried on swiftly through the door and across the hall and through the open door of her bedroom.

'Hardly to be classed as attempted murder,' said Laurie lightly. 'Just a general desire to cause havoc wherever possible. Like mixing up those pills. Wouldn't you say?'

'Are you all right?' asked Brenda anxiously.

'This time I am,' replied Laurie with great emphasis on the 'this'.

They stared at each other for a moment without speaking. Then Mrs Merriman's voice could be heard calling from her room. 'Hurry up, girl! What are you waiting for? I said I wanted to get into my bed.'

Brenda made an anguished grimace. 'I've got to help her,' she said wretchedly. 'There are some things she can't manage alone.'

'I don't believe it,' said Laurie. 'I don't believe there's anything she can't do if she wants to. It's just like Dr Forrest said. The queens can move anywhere.'

Brenda, who was no chess player, gave him a puzzled look and then ran out of the room.

And the pawns had better get out of her way if they don't want to be wiped off the board, added Laurie to himself; though they've not got much freedom of movement, poor little devils. He stood thinking for a moment and then came to a decision. With Romola out of the house and safe in bed in a comfortable nursing home, he could go into her room on the first floor and use the telephone extension there.

Romola's bedroom was rather an austere-looking room, its chief colours being olive green and the deep brown of dark mahogany. There was a handsome bookcase and writing desk, but few signs of any specifically feminine occupation. The bed was made and the room in order. Mrs Ransome, the daily help, had performed her usual morning's work while Romola was receiving emergency treatment at the nursing home.

The telephone extension was on the bedside table and Laurie picked up the receiver and dialled what he thought was the right number. A sound like the roar of aircraft assailed his ear. He swore and dropped the receiver and then lifted it again, but before he could dial he heard a far pleasanter sound, Brenda's voice saying, 'Hullo – who's that?'

'Me,' said Laurie, 'trying to get Terence Toogood to contact the nursing agency for us. We've simply got to get someone in to take over here, but I thought the request would come better from a senior member of the university than from a student. You know what people are like about students.'

Brenda agreed that it was a good idea to get TT to do the arranging. 'But I'm ringing him in any case,' she added. 'Mrs Merriman's asked me to.'

'Oho! She has, has she? Not for the same purpose, I imagine.'

'She wants him to come and see her urgently.'

'Right. I'll get off the line. We'll nab him when he comes so that she doesn't get in first with her story of why Romola is sick.'

By waiting on the front doorstep Laurie did in fact succeed in speaking to Terence before Mrs Merriman did, but it was not to much purpose because Terence was too impatient to listen very carefully to what was inevitably a long and complicated narrative, however skilled one might be in the art of précis.

'No evidence at all,' he said. 'Just like that nonsense with the car and the wheelchair. Romola could deliberately have swallowed the wrong pills to make it seem as if her mother was at fault. Two can play at that game. Let me in now, Laurence. She will have heard me come and be suspicious if she's kept waiting.'

Feeling more and more disillusioned and disappointed, Laurie put his key in the door and opened it. Terence went straight to Mrs Merriman's room and Brenda joined Laurie in the drawing-room.

'They none of them want to know when it comes to the crunch,' he said bitterly. 'They're all scared of her. Dr Forrest has neatly removed himself from the scene, and I bet TT is going to do the same. Leaving you and me holding the baby. If only it were a baby and not a wicked old witch.'

'We'll ask him to phone the nursing agency for us,' said Brenda soothingly. 'Surely he can't refuse to do that. After all, he's an old friend of the family. And perhaps he'll be able to persuade Mrs Merriman to let herself be looked after by an agency nurse.'

'I doubt it,' said Laurie gloomily, 'but we might as well have a few more minutes of hoping. If some responsible person doesn't come and take over this whole set-up soon then I'm going to do an Othello act and smother the old woman with a pillow and that will be the end of it.'

Somewhat to Laurie's surprise Brenda looked neither shocked nor reproachful when he uttered this extravagant threat.

'It wouldn't really be all that difficult,' she said. 'I could do it myself.'

Laurie stared at her.

'But I'm not going to,' she added, 'and neither are you. We are both going to leave this house with Mrs Merriman still alive and in charge of somebody responsible. That's our aim, isn't it, Laurie?'

'That's our aim, love. I only wish I could see how it is to be realized.'

CHAPTER XVIII

WHEN TERENCE came into the drawing-room some time later Laurie and Brenda were seated side by side on the settee, taking stock of their financial resources and discussing the possibility of getting another flat.

'I am making some phone calls for her,' said Terence, 'and she wants some tea, Brenda. So do I.'

His manner of speaking was still very abrupt. Terence Toogood was definitely not in the best of tempers.

'She's probably been giving him a few home truths as she did Dr Forrest,' said Laurie when he had followed Brenda into the kitchen. 'By the way, Bren, how do you like being ordered about as if you were an old-time parlourmaid?'

'It's not as bad as the snack bar,' said Brenda, 'but I don't think I'll go into domestic service. Though I wouldn't mind training as a nurse.'

'Then you shall, darling, you shall. Pity you didn't do a science degree and not an arts. You'll have all that physiology to do. But you'll get a grant. And I'll stop all this nonsense about giving up my D.Phil. and we'll both be students again for a couple of years. Lazy and ir-responsible students, spending all the taxpayers' money and giving nothing in return.'

Laurie did a little dance round the kitchen because it was so wonderful to feel all right with Brenda again. Then he came to a sudden stop and added gloomily: 'If ever we get out of this bloody house. Shall I go and ring that nursing place myself?'

'I think we'd better wait to see what Terence is doing,' said Brenda, pouring water into the teapot. 'He may be doing it himself.'

She was right. Terence Toogood put down the tele-phone receiver as they came out of the kitchen, each carrying a tray, and said with a return to his usual friendliness: 'There'll be a woman coming in from an agency to take over everything tomorrow morning. So if you two could just carry on for one more night it would be a great kindness. And there will be someone coming in to see her on business in about fifteen minutes' time. I'm afraid that will probably mean yet more tea, Brenda,' he added before he followed Laurie into the drawing-room.

'Sorry about all this, Laurence,' he said when the door was shut behind them, 'but it is quite definitely coming to an end tomorrow. For you two at any rate. I think the best thing then is for you both to come to stay with me until you've found another flat. It might not be all that difficult during vacation.'

Laurie made a noncommittal reply. Presumably this was a genuine offer, but it had none of the warmth and urgency of TT's previous invitation to himself alone, and he had more than ever the feeling that the older man wanted only to be rid of Beechcroft and all its works for ever, just as Dr Forrest had wanted. They were all of them, he decided, in their hearts frightened of Mrs Merriman. As indeed he was himself, though probably for a different reason.

'Who is this person coming to see her on business?' he asked a little later, after the front doorbell had rung and Brenda had been heard to let in the visitor.

'Her solicitor,' said Terence crisply. 'In true classic whodunit style she has sent for her solicitor. No prizes for guessing the reason.'

'Cutting Romola out of her will, I suppose,' said Laurie. It was in fact the first time that he had seriously considered the financial aspects of the situation at Beechcroft.

'Romola and others,' said Terence.

Laurie glanced up at this very donnish-looking man whom he had always liked. Was it possible that he too had had expectations? That he had never neglected the office of a friend of the family for reasons other than of pure benevolence?

'How much money has she got to leave?' asked Laurie in his blunt way. 'I didn't know that academics ever made fortunes in Professor Merriman's time, before the days of telly-dons.'

'My dear Laurence,' replied Terence, 'have you forgotten your liberated ladies? The Married Women's Property Act was passed quite a number of decades before Patience Merriman inherited her father's money. He was a manufacturer of patent medicines and she was an only child. She has never stinted herself, nor Romola either, in the matter of purely material comforts. That much justice one must do her. I have a suspicion they have been delving into capital lately, but even so I should guess there is still plenty left.'

So Professor Francis Merriman had married a rich wife, thought Laurie. No doubt the fact had contributed towards his neglect of his own daughter. In this Laurie did the late Professor Merriman an injustice, but he was in a mood to be disillusioned with everybody. Cowardice, compromise, and refusal to face unpleasant facts seemed to him to be all around him. No doubt even Romola, for whom he still felt sympathy and admiration, would turn out to have had an ulterior motive for sticking to her mother.

And for murdering her. But in fact she had not murdered her, and if Dr Forrest was as good as his word, she would have no opportunity to do so. Neither would he. They were out of it. Without any of the money.

'Who do you think she will leave it to instead?' asked Laurie.

'The proverbial cats' home, no doubt,' replied Terence,

and immediately proceeded to talk about Laurie's subject of research. Twenty minutes later, when the door of the drawing-room opened and the face of a strange man appeared, Terence's impromptu lecture was still in full flow.

'I'm sorry to interrupt you,' said the newcomer, 'but I wonder if I could trouble you to come and witness Mrs Merriman's signature. You are Dr Toogood and Mr Kingston, aren't you?'

He was a plump, bald, worried-looking little man, and Terence greeted him in a patronizing manner that grated on Laurie.

'Your assumption is correct, Mr Edwards. It was I who spoke to your office some thirty-five minutes ago.' He turned to Laurie. 'That answers part of your question, Laurence. Witnesses to the signature cannot be beneficiaries. You and I are out of it this time, my lad.'

Laurie gave a feeble little laugh in reply. None of the things that he would have liked to say seemed appropriate to the moment. 'Where's Brenda?' he asked as they all three came out into the hall.

Nobody answered, and he repeated the question to Mrs Merriman when he came into the bedroom.

'I sent her to do some shopping for me,' was the reply.

'But it's nearly six o'clock. The shops will be shut,' objected Laurie.

'Do you think we could get on with the business,' said Mr Edwards impatiently. He turned to Mrs Merriman, who was propped up against a wall of pillows, looking very small and frail and lying very still, apparently in patient resignation. But her face belied her attitude. Though the lips were motionless, the eyes were alert and active, missing nothing, neither the boy's anxiety, nor the lawyer's annoyance at being summoned just when he was about to finish his working day, nor the wariness behind the steel-rimmed glasses and smooth façade of her old friend Terence Toogood.

Here were three men of varying age and experience, all active in mind and body, all with considerable ability in their respective ways, and yet they were all in awe of her. She had them in her power.

Patience Merriman was enjoying herself enormously. Never had she imagined, when she wrote that fake diary entry in order to get something happening around her on which she could exert her powers of intrigue and relieve her boredom, that such wonderful dramas would result. True, she had lost Romola for the moment, but she still had the youngsters, and even if she had not succeeded yet in driving a firm wedge between them, there were other ways in which she could work mischief. She had one already in mind, and as for that housekeeper woman who would be turning up tomorrow, Mrs Merriman had no doubt at all that she would very soon be able to get rid of *her*.

Meanwhile the triumph over that smooth customer Geoffrey Forrest had been most delightful. Fancy him having had his eyes on Romola's inheritance all this time! She ought to have seen it before; it was rare for something like that to escape her notice, but she had put that right now in the codicil to her will that she was just about to sign. The fool of a lawyer had wanted to leave it till tomorrow and get it typed in the office, but she was determined to execute it today. Handwriting was as binding as typing: the signature was all that mattered. At the rate things were happening, or rather, at the rate Mrs Merriman was determined to make them happen, tomorrow might well be too late.

She had two alternative schemes for the next piece of drama. If one of them failed there would always be the other. This other was rather in the nature of a time-bomb, and unfortunately she herself would not be there to see it go off. But it was amusing to dwell on the effects in her mind, and she could always change the plan if she thought of something better.

'I think you will have to find me something firmer to write on,' she said with an air of weary resignation. 'I have so little strength in my fingers now.'

There was a general movement among the other three and Mrs Merriman watched them with amusement. It was Laurie who thought of taking the teapot and cup off the tea-tray that lay on the dressing-table and turning the tray upside down to make a table for Mrs Merriman's lap. In fact there was a perfectly good bed-table folded up and standing in the corner of the room by the wardrobe, but none of them knew about it or noticed it, and Mrs Merriman would not have dreamed of telling them.

'Thank you,' she said to Laurie. 'What a clever boy you are!'

Much to his own annoyance, Laurie could feel himself flushing with frustrated fury. Mr Edwards produced the sheet of paper on which he had written the necessary clauses and placed it on the upturned tray.

'No, no, not that thing!' cried Mrs Merriman in disgust as he tried to hand her a ballpoint pen. 'I can't write with that modern rubbish. Where is my fountain pen? The gold one that I always use.'

Her three attendants looked at each other helplessly, and Laurie decided that Mrs Merriman had sent Brenda off on some pointless errand purely so that there would be nobody left in the house who knew where she kept her belongings, thus causing the maximum of delay, frustration, and general irritation among those who were obliged to attend to her commands.

Again it was Laurie who came to the rescue. He had often seen Mrs Merriman's face at the drawing-room window when he came into the house. This was where she usually sat, and presumably she would do her writing at the table there, a gate-legged table of dark oak, of which one flap was kept permanently raised.

'I think I know where it is,' he muttered and ran out of the room. He found the pen lying alongside a gold pencil in a glass tray that stood on the window-sill beyond the oak table. There was also a cheaper black fountain pen and he picked up the whole tray, together with a bottle of ink standing near, since he was quite sure that Mrs Merriman would be delighted to find an excuse for sending him back to fetch something else. As it was, however, she was obliged to content herself with saying that he had no need to bring a whole stationer's shop with him and with increasing her own determination to get her own back on this young man before very much more time had elapsed.

Laurie was, in fact, posing quite a problem to Patience. He could not be taunted in the way that she had taunted Geoffrey Forrest and Terence Toogood, nor was it possible to work her poor old lady act with him. However, even Laurie had his weak spots. The chief of them was at this very moment cycling halfway across Oxford at Mrs Merriman's request to have an old prescription made up for her at a chemist's that stayed open late. Mrs Merriman didn't really want the prescription at all: it was for a mild tonic, nothing to frighten anybody with, but she wanted Brenda right out of the way for an hour, as Laurie had guessed.

The signing of the paper took some time. It was a long while since Patience Merriman had altered her will and she had rather forgotten what pleasure there was to be derived from it. Of course the pleasure depended on having some expectant people around you, and most of the distant relatives and others who had once had expectations had long since either abandoned them or decided that it was not worth putting up with Mrs Merriman for the sake of a possible legacy. However, she could always collect some more around her, and there was always Romola to fall back on when all else failed. Romola would be very chastened when she came home again. She must have had a bad fright over those tablets – who would have thought that the little scheme would have worked so well? – and with Geoffrey Forrest fading out of the picture when he heard of Romola being disinherited, the silly girl would have to come to heel when her mother called her. Meanwhile there were the youngsters to play with, and she was going to need quite a lot of her energy to deal with that game, so she had better not drag out this scene any longer but do the signing now and get rid of them all and have a little rest.

'There you are,' she said as if bestowing a great favour upon her listeners, and she produced a very firm signature with a fine flourish of the 'P' of the Patience.

Mr Edwards, holding a piece of blotting paper over the writing above the signature, held the upturned tray for first Terence and then Laurie to add their own names.

'Now clear out, the lot of you,' said Mrs Merriman as if the three of them had been insisting on lingering there against her will instead of trying to conceal their longing to get away. 'Clear out and leave me in peace.'

The solicitor was out of the room first, reflecting that he might with luck be home in time to watch his favourite television programme, after all. Terence made a slightly more prolonged farewell, turned to Laurie and said, 'You know my number if you need me,' and then disappeared too.

Laurie remained till the last. He stood three feet away from the bed, looking down on Mrs Merriman. She was lying back against the pillows again and her eyes were closed.

'Where's Brenda?' he asked.

Patience Merriman made no reply and did not stir.

'Where's Brenda?' said Laurie again.

Again there was no response.

Laurie looked at the shrunken figure in the pink night-gown and bed-jacket, at the white hair and the lines in the face and the twisted fingers lying on the sheet. It would not be difficult, he said to himself. All he need do was hold one of those pillows over her face for a little while. She would try clawing at him no doubt but she would not be able to get out of bed. There probably wouldn't even be any bruises on her, nor any sign of what had happened. It would look as if she had had a heart attack. And even if Dr Geoffrey Forrest did suspect or guess what had taken place, it was unlikely in the extreme that he would ever say so. The death certificate would be impeccable. After all, Laurie would only have been doing the doctor's own dirty work for him.

Laurie stood and looked down at Mrs Merriman and thought about it for a full minute before he too turned and left the room.

CHAPTER XIX

BRENDA WAS NOT in the top flat, but Laurie had not really expected that she would be, so he was not unduly disappointed. He wasted no time looking elsewhere in the house but went out to the shed by the garage to see if her bike was gone, which it was. That reassured him: it was simply a case of waiting until she returned from her errands. For a moment he thought of going for a walk or a ride himself to shake some of the horrible oppression of Beechcroft away, but decided against it partly because he wanted to be there when Brenda got back and partly because, in spite of everything, it did not seem right to leave the old woman alone in the house.

Laurie smiled at himself as he wandered round to the back garden. One moment he was seriously thinking of murdering her and the next moment he was worrying about leaving her alone in the house in case she came to some harm. How absurd could you get?

It had been another day of alternate sunshine and showers, and at the moment the sun was shining on the wet leaves and petals of the rose hedge that separated the kitchen garden from the lawn. Suddenly, for no apparent reason except that it felt so good to be away from the house and out here sniffing the freshness of the wet earth and the glistening roses, Laurie found himself feeling light-hearted and cheerful as he had not felt for some time. Brenda would be back soon, and he and Brenda were now perfectly all right again together, and they would find somewhere else to live, without the advantages of Beechcroft but without its drawbacks too, and all the world was in front of them and the future was theirs. Those tentacles of Mrs Merriman's ill will, which held everybody in the house in an inescapable grip, did not stretch out into the bright and scented garden. No wonder poor Romola had liked to be out here. It was a haven from which one could even feel it in one's heart to pity the old woman.

This elevated mood lasted Laurie while he inspected the runner-beans and treated himself to a few late raspberries and played hide-and-seek with the neighbour's cat round the apple tree. Some of the mood even remained with him when he walked back round the side of the house to the front drive, although on this spot the shadow cast by the ugly red-brick building was not purely a physical one. Laurie had never really liked the place, even before he had begun to suspect something of Mrs Merriman's true nature, but the temptation of the pleasant little home at the top had been overwhelming. Anyway it was nearly over now, and he and Brenda would be closer than ever for the experience. All they had to do now was to get through tonight and then pack up their things and go round to TT's place, leaving Beechcroft behind for ever, except that Laurie thought he would like to keep in touch with Romola. It would be wonderful if Dr Forrest really did stick to her, even without the money, but Laurie was feeling so disillusioned about these older men that he didn't think this was very likely.

Sadness for Romola vanished, however, when he saw Brenda turn in at the gate. He ran forward from where he had been hanging about round the side of the shed and they met in the drive just under the window of Mrs

Merriman's bedroom. Brenda let her bike slip from her hands on to the gravel and they clung to each other as if it were the first time they had ever done so and as if they could never let go. And in both of their minds, mixed with this almost desperate joy, was the remembrance of their first meeting in Magpie Lane.

Mrs Merriman, who had got out of bed and was sitting in her chair by the window of her bedroom contemplating her next move, saw the two young people rush into each other's arms and remain there oblivious of everything around them. All the triumph of her afternoon's work turned to dust and ashes. Her eyes dilated with hatred and fury, her mouth began its uncontrollable champing, and her knotted hands twisted together. The sight of the two young people was horrible to her, bitter almost beyond belief. It was as if somebody was forcing a cup of gall down her throat and she was choking.

After a few minutes the worst of the spasms passed and her mind was able to work again. She decided that she would make some modification to her plan, for this situation called for even more drastic measures than she had devised. Thinking out ways and means brought her some relief, and by the time Brenda came in to see whether she was all right and whether she needed anything, Mrs Merriman was back in bed and able to answer in a convincingly sleepy manner.

'No, thank you, my dear. Not just yet. I'm rather tired, with all those people and all that business. I will rest till supper-time, and then perhaps I will get up for a little while and you shall make me a meal. Something light like an omelette. You make such delicious omelettes, dear Brenda.'

Mrs Merriman paused for a moment. She was afraid that she might have been overdoing the sweetness. One tended to do so when one's mind was burning up with hatred. A return to her brisker manner might be advisable now.

'And after that,' she said, 'when you've cleared up and got me back to bed again I am going to send you off duty because it's time you had a break from me. I'll take some of this medicine you've kindly fetched for me – it always used to put me right in the old days before they started on all these modern poisons – and I'm quite sure I shall sleep like a top. So off you go now and attend to your young man for a bit. I'm afraid I've made you neglect him shamefully these last days. Oh, and Brenda, my dear.'

Brenda paused at the door of the room.

'If you would do just one more thing for me now, and that is, telephone the nursing home and find out how Romola is. I meant to ask Terence to do it, but we had so much business to conclude, and he gets very impatient at times. You wouldn't think it would be such a great hardship to him to give up a couple of hours when you think of all that my husband did for him. However, off he went and I didn't feel up to telephoning myself.'

'Would you like me to plug the extension from the other room in here,' said Brenda, 'so that you can speak to them yourself?'

'No, thank you. It's only to make sure she is all right and that there has not been any relapse.'

Mrs Merriman felt that she really ought to express some sympathy for her daughter in order to make the act more convincing, but did not feel up to it at the moment. Asking Brenda to telephone would have to suffice.

'She's quite comfortable,' said Brenda returning to the

room a few minutes later. 'She's been sleeping for some hours.'

'Whom did you speak to?' asked Mrs Merriman.

'I'm not quite sure. I think it was the matron,' replied Brenda.

This was a lie and Brenda was not very good at lying. In fact the call had been answered by one of the nurses, who had put Brenda straight through to Dr Forrest at the sound of the name 'Merriman'. It turned out that he was sitting by Romola's bedside.

'If you are being overheard,' he had said immediately he found out who it was, 'then don't say anything aloud except yes. Tell Romola's mother that she is quite comfortable – which she is, truly – and don't let on that I am here. And don't forget – if you or Laurence needs me, then he has got my phone numbers.'

'The matron?' Mrs Merriman looked keenly at Brenda. 'Was that all she said?'

'Just that she was comfortable,' repeated Brenda.

'Had she had any visitors?'

'They didn't say. Do you want me to ring again to find out?'

This was quite a clever move. Even the most truthful and straightforward of people tended to acquire a little deviousness after close association with Mrs Merriman. Brenda was learning at last.

'No, thank you,' said Mrs Merriman. 'That would look rather foolish, wouldn't it? As if I didn't know who would be likely to be taking an interest in the well-being of my own daughter! Run along now.'

Brenda ran, most gratefully.

'I don't know what to make of it,' she said to Laurie in the top flat a minute later. 'I'm sure she guessed Dr

Forrest was with Romola.'

'I can tell you exactly what to make of it,' said Laurie, and he proceeded to give her a full account of the signing of the will that had taken place during Brenda's absence from the house.

'Who d'you think she's left the money to, then?' asked Brenda.

They were sitting at the table in their living-room, eating the cold meats and salad that Laurie had brought in earlier in the day. It seemed ages since they had last had a meal together and they both ate with excellent appetites.

'Heaven knows,' said Laurie. 'TT suggested the proverbial cattery.'

'But she doesn't like cats,' objected Brenda.

'Don't be so literal, sweetie. For cats' home read charities in general.'

'I don't think she would do that,' said Brenda thoughtfully, helping herself to a fourth slice of bread and butter. 'It would be too boring and impersonal. She loves controlling people too much for that. She'd like to think she was causing somebody trouble with her will even if she wasn't there to see it.'

Laurie beamed at her. 'Well done, love. You're getting her measure at long last. Never ignore the slightest possibility of making mischief. That's our delightful old lady friend. Never mind. It hasn't worked with us.' And he got up and danced round the table before coming to a stop behind Brenda's chair and flinging his arms around her neck. 'Here's two little flies who have got away from the web. Or will be away tomorrow.'

'Suppose the woman from the agency doesn't turn up,' said Brenda.

'Then Terence will have to find somebody else. It's more his job than ours. Or he can damned well move in and look after her himself. I wish you didn't have to go down again tonight.' Laurie rubbed his cheek against the top of Brenda's head. 'Why don't we just leave her alone? She can't come to any harm then and nor can we. We'll barricade ourselves in.'

'She did say I was to go off duty after I'd got her supper,' said Brenda, 'so I suppose I could stay up here and not sleep on the settee. What do you think, Laurie?'

'I think you're daft. Has she paid you anything yet for being a twenty-four hours a day attendant slave?'

'Not yet,' admitted Brenda.

'How much did you arrange to be paid?'

'Well, actually we never got round to fixing it. But she keeps hinting that I'll be well recompensed.'

Laurie groaned and made extravagant gestures of despair. 'You're not going to get a penny. You've been conned. And you've nothing in writing, so you can whistle for your wages. Never mind. Put it all down to experience. You will leave this house a sadder and a wiser woman.'

'As long as I leave this house alive,' said Brenda, 'I don't care how else I leave it.'

For a few minutes they clung together and then Laurie said: 'Let's go to bed now, Bren. Don't go down again.'

'But I've promised to get her some supper.'

'Damn. I suppose there's no use trying to persuade you to let the old harridan stew in her own poisonous potions? No? I thought so. All right then. I'll come too.'

'She won't like it,' demurred Brenda.

'Then she can do the other thing. Where is she going to eat?'

'In the sitting-room, I expect. She said she'd like to sit up for a bit.'

'Then I'll stay in the kitchen,' said Laurie. 'You needn't let on that I'm there. If she shows signs of coming in, I'll go out into the garden. I've no more wish to see her than she has to see me but I want to be downstairs so long as you are. For God's sake have a good look at everything you're using for cooking and don't let her go handing you any more pills to swallow, whatever she says. Promise me, Brenda.'

Brenda promised.

'And call me if you have the least bit of trouble. Promise.'

'I don't know,' said Brenda doubtfully. 'Suppose you went and lost your temper with her and did something.'

'I don't go and *do* things!' cried Laurie indignantly. 'I may feel like it but I never do it. Since when have you looked on me as a representative of the violent and un-controlled youth of today?'

'Senseless violence,' said Brenda. 'No, darling, that's not you at all. But this is different. Mrs Merriman could drive a saint to murder if she really put her mind to it.'

'I'm not a saint and I'm not going to do anything rash,' said Laurie. 'I just want you to call me if you have any trouble with her. All I shall do is drag you away because you won't be able to drag yourself. Right?'

'Right,' said Brenda. 'If you'll promise to stick to that, then I'll promise too.'

Neither of these promises was put to the test, however, while Mrs Merriman was being served with her omelette at the table by the window in the sitting-room. Her sweet little old lady act never faltered for a second, and it evoked a similar but less efficient display of insincerity from Brenda. The girl felt sickened with herself as she smiled at Mrs Merriman and asked whether she would like a peach peeled for her. Part of the revulsion was at the sheer hypocrisy of it, a quality that Brenda had come to detest more and more since she had come to know and love Laurie. But part of it was a disgust with herself for not having seen through Mrs Merriman before. Laurie had been right about her all along, and she, Brenda, had been taken in and was therefore partly responsible for the fact that Romola Merriman had been so ill and was probably losing her inheritance and that Laurie had been so anxious and wretched.

Brenda was a girl who always had to feel a bit guilty about somebody or something, and by the time she had helped Mrs Merriman back to bed again, she was not only feeling guilty about Romola and Laurie, but was even beginning to feel a little flicker of pity for the old woman again, not because Mrs Merriman was a poor feeble invalid, but because she must surely be bitterly unhappy at heart, loving nobody and being loved by nobody.

'If you will leave the glass just there where I can easily reach it,' said Mrs Merriman to Brenda after the girl had poured some red liquid out of the bottle she had collected from the chemist, 'then I will take it when I need it. I'm not taking any more of Geoffrey Forrest's pills. We'll get that young colleague of his in to see me tomorrow. She's a charming girl. Rather like you, my dear. A nice, sensible, understanding sort of girl.'

'Is there anything else you'd like me to do?' asked Brenda. She found it particularly embarrassing when Mrs

Merriman made these personal remarks. That they were totally insincere she now had no doubt, but she still had no conception of the full measure of the old woman's hatred for her.

'No, thank you. I am perfectly comfortable now,' was the reply.

'I'll look in then,' said Brenda, 'before I make up my bed.'

'You will do no such thing,' said Mrs Merriman with a little flash of her imperious manner. 'I am not having you put yourself to any more trouble on my behalf. I told you so earlier. I shall be perfectly all right now and you are to go upstairs to your young man.'

'I don't like to think you've got nobody within call,' said Brenda doubtfully.

'Oh, very well then,' said Mrs Merriman with an impatient little movement of her hands as if she were being persuaded against her better judgement, 'if you are really all that worried about me, then you had better leave the door of the top flat open. You'll be able to hear me then if I call out loudly enough, and I've also got my little brass bell. Will that satisfy you, Brenda?'

Brenda indicated that it would.

'Then kiss me good night and be off with you. And don't think I don't appreciate what you've done for me. I have not forgotten you. You will be recompensed for all your pains. Good night, my dear.'

Since there was no way to avoid it Brenda leaned over and brushed the old woman's cheek with her lips. It felt surprisingly soft and tender, almost like a baby's skin.

'Good night,' she said. 'Sleep well.'

Five minutes later she was telling Laurie about it.

'The kiss of Judas,' he said.

'Oh Laurie, what can she do to us? What harm can she possibly do to us now?' cried Brenda.

'I don't know,' he replied, frowning. 'I only know I shan't feel safe till we've gone.'

'Well, what do you want us to do now?' asked Brenda. 'Shall we go and sit on the front doorstep all night? Or in the shed? I don't mind doing that if that's what you want. We could take it in turns to doze a bit.'

Laurie looked for a moment as if he was going to fall in with this suggestion. It was what they ought to do: he knew it himself. Caution and intellect both said that it was the right course. But youth and nature and the presence of Brenda, warm and loving and all his own, revolted.

'No, dammit!' he cried. 'Not now I've got you back at last. Let's go to bed.'

Two floors down Mrs Merriman was smiling to herself as she pictured with a fair degree of accuracy the scene that was taking place in the attic flat. Everything was going perfectly according to plan. The door of the flat would be left open, she felt sure. Any loud sound would be audible up there but not a softer sound. Both young people were suspicious and on their guard by now and they might well discuss the possibility of taking precautions. But they had been kept apart for some time and in the end the urge of young blood would be too strong for them. In their great need to find comfort in each other's arms lay their great weakness. In Patience Merriman's utter loneliness and the lack of any hope or meaning in her life lay her great strength.

She rested a little with closed eyes but ears alert for any sign of movement in the house. Then she looked at her watch and decided it was still rather too early. An hour later she got carefully out of bed and into the chair, felt in her dressing-gown pocket to make sure she had everything she needed, and then ran the chair silently out into the hall. The house was eerily quiet. She ran the chair into the drawing-room to check that there was nobody there, then into the kitchen, just in case her ears should have deceived her and one of them had slipped downstairs after all. The cloakroom and the small junk room adjoining it were the next to be inspected. They were unlikely places, but she was determined to make quite sure. After that came the most difficult part of the whole enterprise, checking that the youngsters were not lurking somewhere on the first floor.

Mrs Merriman assembled all her reserves for the silent crawl up the big staircase. She did it backwards, sitting on each step in turn as she raised herself up. It took a long time but it saved her strength for the later tasks, and it was also much the quietest way to progress. When she got to the first-floor landing she crawled, tucking her nightgown and dressing-gown up around her hips. She had made use of this manner of progression before now when she was alone in the house and wanted to go upstairs. It was not as speedy as with the chair, but it was not much slower than a normal person's walk and it was infinitely better than trusting to her uncertain legs that could let her down at a vital moment with a noisy crash.

When she had finished checking on the first floor of Beechcroft she returned to the big staircase and rested on the top step. She was tired but by no means completely at an end of her resources. Not a sound came from the attic floor. Mrs Merriman prepared herself to move again. All had gone completely according to plan so far and now came the most important moment of all.

CHAPTER XX

IT WAS about a quarter to three when Brenda woke. She had been in a deep sleep and it was several seconds before she became conscious that the sounds she was hearing were actually coming to her ears and were not part of her dream. They were high-pitched sounds, definitely human in origin and equally definitely coming from somebody in distress. Brenda sat up and turned her head to look at Laurie's sleeping form, just visible in the dimness of the room. Laurie sometimes talked in his sleep and even moaned a little, but he never made this sort of noise.

It came again. This time it was clearly distinguishable as a cry for help, and it was followed by a muffled thump as if something or somebody had fallen to the floor.

'Oh my God, she's had a stroke or something!' cried Brenda to herself, and her reaction was as automatic as leaping out of the way of a fast-approaching car. You heard someone crying for help and you rushed to help them. It was as simple as that. You could not stop yourself.

Brenda got out of the bed and thumped Laurie on the back. 'She's had an accident or something,' she said. 'We'll have to go. Hurry up.'

Laurie stirred and grunted and then immediately went back to sleep again.

'We've got to go down.' Brenda thumped him again. 'She's yelling for help.'

The cries were becoming more desperate now.

'Do wake up, Laurie!' Brenda shook him and he sat up at last, blinking and struggling into consciousness. 'I'm going,' she added as she ran to the door. 'Come on.'

'Hi – wait for me!' cried Laurie, fully awake at last. He threw back the bedclothes and ran after her, reaching the bottom of the attic stairs as Brenda got to the head of the main staircase. She had switched on the lights as she ran, and he could see her turn from the first-floor landing on to the top stair. After that she was out of his line of vision for the two or three seconds it took him to run along the passage.

It was during these very few seconds that he heard the crash – a tremendous crash, resounding through the house. Then all was silent: no sound of movement, no cries for help. In the split second before Laurie reached the top of the big flight of stairs it flashed through his mind that Mrs Merriman must have been in trouble after all to have caused such a tremendous crash and Brenda had been right to investigate. That was his half-formed mental image, as the stairs and the hall came into view: the old woman lying injured on the floor and Brenda leaning over her.

The reality was so different that for a moment he could not take it in. He stood on the turn of the staircase, looking down on a scene that was to stay in his mind for the rest of his life. There was indeed a human figure crumpled up on the floor at the foot of the stairs and there was another one bending over it. But the one on the floor had thick dark hair and the one bending over was seated in a wheelchair.

Laurie let out a loud yell of horror and fury, flung himself over the wide rail of the banisters and slid down it, took a great leap over Brenda's motionless body, caught hold of the back of the wheelchair and pushed it away from him with great violence. There was a faint cry and then another crash. He did not even look round to see what had happened but knelt down beside Brenda and cried her name. She was all in a heap with her head touching the floor and both legs crumpled up beneath her. The eyes were closed and the face was deathly pale but there was no sign of blood. Nor was there any sign of movement. Laurie felt the full weight of the sickness of despair before he felt the faint heartbeat in Brenda's body.

He got up and rushed to the telephone and dialled Dr Forrest's home number, still with eyes for nothing but Brenda.

Dr Forrest did not waste any time in unnecessary questions. 'Don't do anything till I come,' was all he said. 'I won't be long.'

Laurie replaced the receiver and returned to where Brenda lay. It was intolerable to feel so helpless, to be able to do nothing for her, but he dared not go against the doctor's advice. To get through those endless leaden minutes before Dr Forrest arrived, he looked up at the staircase to see how Brenda had fallen and what he saw made him once more cry out aloud.

Just before the turn of the stairs and about eight or nine steps up from the hall the carpet was lying slack and twisted over two of the treads. The reason for this was instantly obvious. The brass rods that held the carpet on these two stairs had come out of their sockets at one end and were lying loose, no longer serving their purpose. Anybody coming downstairs, whether quickly or slowly, whether the light was good or bad, could hardly fail to slip and fall, and the two loose rods, one after the other, made it a virtual certainty that the fall would be a bad one. If Laurie had come down the stairs himself just now instead of sliding down the banisters to save time, he would at this moment be lying injured too, because in his hurry to reach Brenda he would certainly not have noticed the loose carpet. And if it had been he and not Brenda who had been the first to descend, then he would have come that headlong crash, and it would have been Brenda rushing after him in horror. And she would not have slid down the banisters so she would have fallen headlong too.

It was the neatest, simplest, and oldest little mantrap in the world, and with all their knowledge of Mrs Merriman they ought not to have fallen into it. It would probably be impossible to prove that she had loosened the stair-rods. Rods did sometimes work loose; accidents like this did sometimes happen. As Dr Forrest had pointed out so strongly, what jury would ever believe that a feeble old lady like that could be capable of planning murder? They would not even believe that she would have the strength to get so far upstairs, let alone slide the rods from their sockets.

But she was not going to get away with it. Whether Brenda lived or died, the old witch was going to pay for her crime. If there was no evidence that she had been on the stairs then he would have to fake some – fingerprints, some item of her clothing – even at a pinch swear that he himself had seen her. As Laurie straightened up from where he had been kneeling just below the loose rods it occurred to him for the first time since he had pushed Mrs Merriman's chair away from Brenda to wonder what had happened to the old woman. He vaguely remembered hearing a crash and since then she had made no sound. Perhaps she was injured too.

He turned round and looked down on the hall. Brenda lay at the foot of the stairs and a few feet beyond her he could see the wheelchair. It was empty and the cushions had fallen out on to the floor. They were dark red cushions and they did not show up very clearly against the predominantly dark red patterned carpet. But something not far from them did show up. It looked like a little heap of pale pink clothing or rags. Laurie's mind, shaken with shock, fury and anxiety, did not fully register what it was. The doorbell rang and he had to step round the pale pink heap in order to get to the front door.

'Good God!' cried Geoffrey Forrest, quickly surveying the scene. 'It looks like the last act of *Hamlet*. What happened?'

Laurie explained quickly while the doctor knelt down beside Brenda.

'I pushed the chair away,' he concluded. 'I'd no idea I pushed it so hard. It must have crashed against the wall and knocked her out. I didn't realize at first. I was only thinking about Brenda. And about how the stair-rods had been loosened.'

Geoffrey Forrest did not comment, but he had taken in all that Laurie was saying and he looked up at the staircase before moving over to kneel down beside the pale pink heap. He remained there only a very short while before getting up again and going to the telephone.

'The old one's dead but the young one's got a chance,' he said to Laurie as he dialled a number.

A little later he said: 'The ambulance won't be long, but I'm afraid I'll have to phone the police. If Brenda should die it will mean an inquest.'

'Am I going to be accused of murdering Mrs Merriman?' asked Laurie rather shakily.

'Not if I can help it,' said the doctor, pausing with his hand over the telephone and looking keenly at the boy.

'You said no court would ever believe she would be guilty of attempted murder,' said Laurie.

The doctor replaced the receiver without dialling a number and came a step towards Laurie. 'Look,' he said, 'would you just leave this to me. I have to ring the police and when the inspector comes I want you to tell him exactly what happened. No theories. No speculation. Exactly what happened. That's all. You don't have to tell any lies whatever. You just leave out all your own ideas about it. Got me?'

'What are you going to do?'

'Exactly the same. Tell the facts and leave out the theories. Let the police draw their own conclusions.'

They stared at each other and then the older man's face softened and he took hold of Laurie by both arms and shook him gently. 'You've had a very bad shock. Go and make yourself some tea. Weak with lots of sugar. It'll do you more good than alcohol. I can't say, don't worry about Brenda. You'll have days and maybe weeks of worry ahead. The bruises and broken legs will heal but concussion's a chancy business. But I've seen people recover from far worse injuries. Hang on to that. Go on now. Make that tea.'

And he gave Laurie a friendly push in the direction of the kitchen before he picked up the receiver again.

It was not so difficult after all, Laurie found, to tell the police inspector the plain truth and nothing more. They sat in the drawing-room, all four of them, the two police officers, Dr Forrest, and Laurie, and the doctor frequently joined in when Laurie was telling his story. Without any lies being told, the general impression was given that the young people really had nothing to do with the household downstairs, but that in the absence of the daughter and in the gap before the housekeeper arrived, they had kindly consented to keep an eye on the old woman. It was not false, but it left out practically everything that mattered.

Dr Forrest was quite a well-known figure in the town. He even knew the inspector slightly from an accident case in which he had given evidence a few months ago. Laurie marvelled at how smoothly the whole story slipped across apparently without the least suspicion that it was not the full truth, although he could not help wondering whether the two stolid and rather bored-looking policemen had any suspicious thoughts that they were keeping to themselves. His own worst moment came when he was asked exactly where Mrs Merriman's chair had been when he got to the foot of the stairs.

'It was right in front of me,' he replied. 'I had to push it out of the way to get to Brenda.'

'And you didn't see how hard you had pushed it? Nor where it went?'

Laurie shook his head. 'I didn't think about it. I only knew I had to get to Brenda. I thought she was dead. And she might be dying now.' He finished with a little gasp, as the reality of this possibility came right home to him at last. The three older men looked at him with some compassion. There was no doubt about the measure of the boy's shock and distress.

Dr Forrest interrupted yet again. 'We've got to keep on hoping, Laurence,' he said. 'I'll ring the hospital again as soon as we've finished here. Would you like me to complete the statement, Inspector?'

'If you would, sir.'

'As we have seen,' said the doctor, 'the chair rolled towards this room and ran into the closed door. Whether Mrs Merriman was still alive at that moment and tried to stop it we shall never know, but my opinion is that she was not.'

Laurie, suddenly remembering the faint moan that he had heard after he had pushed the chair away, was about to interrupt but stopped just in time. Had he mentioned the moan to Dr Forrest? Did the doctor seriously believe that the old woman was dead or dying before she fell? Or was it all a cover-up to save Laurie from any possible suspicion of manslaughter?

'In any case she would have been much too weak to stop the movement,' continued Geoffrey Forrest smoothly, giving the merest glance in Laurie's direction. 'She must have used up the last of her resources in calling out for help.'

'She would have been having some sort of attack?' suggested the inspector.

Dr Forrest produced a battery of medical information and the eyes of his three hearers took on a rather glazed look. Laurie found himself doubting the evidence of his own senses and his own reasoning. Could that moan have come from Brenda and not from Mrs Merriman at all?

'So you think the old lady had been trying to get upstairs?' said the police inspector when Dr Forrest had done.

'I would imagine so. She was not totally immobile. She could walk a little if absolutely necessary. Of course this is all speculation – ' and again the doctor glanced at Laurie as if to ensure his silence – 'but it seems to me the most likely reason for the accident. I would think that

Mrs Merriman felt ill during the night and rang the electric bell for her daughter, forgetting that she was not there. She might have tried ringing the little brass bell hoping one of the young people would hear, or she might have forgotten about it and started trying to get upstairs to them. That would account for the piece of pink feather on the staircarpet. It must have been rubbed off the neck of the bed-jacket as she crawled up – for she could only do it by crawling.'

The doctor did not glance at Laurie as he spoke these last words, but the boy could feel the underlying command in his voice. Dr Forrest was telling him, as plainly as if he had spoken aloud, to keep quiet. Laurie was not to be allowed to speculate, but Geoffrey Forrest could and would do so in spite of what he had said. And it was not confined to speculation. Laurie was quite sure that there had been no piece of pale pink fluff clinging to the staircarpet where the rods had come loose when he himself had inspected the spot before the doctor's arrival. The piece of trimming from the bed-jacket had got there since, and there was only one way in which it could have got there. Laurie himself had only thought of faking evidence: Geoffrey Forrest had actually done it.

Had he done anything else in that brief interval while Laurie was making tea in the kitchen? Moved Mrs Merriman's body? Shifted the chair? Laurie could not tell. He was becoming confused himself now. With a feeling of helplessness, combined with a certain amount of resentment against the doctor, he heard Dr Forrest continue.

'I should say that is probably what happened, and that she either crawled or slipped back again and got back into the chair and began to cry out for help from there. I may be wrong, of course,' he added with the air of an expert who is perfectly sure that he can never be wrong, 'but I would say that is how the piece of bed-jacket got there.'

'What about the loose stair-rods?' asked the inspector.

Geoffrey Forrest gave an eloquent little shrug. 'I've no idea. Stair-rods do work loose sometimes. She might have got hold of one of them while she was trying to get upstairs and pulled it out. They have a daily cleaning woman, I believe. No doubt she would be able to tell you whether there were any loose rods or any that were liable to come loose.'

So he's going to stick to the accident line, said Laurie to himself, and not try to accuse the old woman of murder. He felt relieved and at the same time disappointed, hating the way the doctor was manipulating the whole business and yet feeling totally unable to take any further part himself. Geoffrey Forrest seemed to be playing a very deep game, but he had acted as quickly and efficiently as any man could over Brenda, and if Brenda's life was saved it would be largely his doing. Not only that, but the misrepresenting of the facts was certainly saving Laurie from any possible unpleasantness. How could Laurie possibly, in the face of such a debt, stick his neck out now and tell the police that Dr Forrest was not keeping strictly to the truth?

Of course he could not. And even if he had tried to, the police would not believe him.

'Mrs Merriman's death was from heart failure, then?' the inspector was saying.

'You could call it that. At any rate, it was from natural causes and not due to the accident of her wheelchair knocking against the wall and tilting her out.'

With these words of Dr Forrest's Laurie again re-

ceived that warning glance that would be interpreted by
anybody else who noticed it as nothing more than a
kindly look.

Perhaps after all it was simply a kindly look. Perhaps it
had all happened exactly as Dr Forrest was suggesting.
What did it all matter anyway if Brenda were going to
die? Accident or murder, no amount of investigation
would bring her back. And as for punishing the guilty,
why, she was already beyond human punishment.

The police officers got up to go at last, thankfully
leaving to Dr Forrest the duty of breaking the news of
Mrs Merriman's death to her next-of-kin, seemingly
quite satisfied with the suggestions put forward by the
doctor, but nevertheless remarking that they had better
see Miss Merriman some time and also the cleaning
woman.

'Miss Merriman will be home tomorrow,' said Geoffrey
Forrest. 'She is having a couple of days' rest in a nursing
home on my advice after a particularly bad bout of
migraine. I don't know the cleaner's name or address,
I'm afraid.'

He looked enquiringly at Laurie, who simply shook his
head.

'But of course Miss Merriman will be able to tell you
that,' continued the doctor. 'And she will probably be
able to tell you about the condition of the stair-rods. I'm
sorry there is nothing more I can do for you.'

'If Miss Long should recover consciousness . . .' began
the inspector.

'Then no doubt she will be able to tell us herself. If
not, then you have all the facts and I will of course make
myself available for the inquest.'

CHAPTER XXI

'Inquest,' said Laurie after the police had gone. 'There won't be any inquest on Mrs Merriman then?'

'Not when death is certified to be of natural causes and when the deceased had been seen by a doctor only a few hours previously.'

'Did you tell all those lies for my sake?'

'I've told no lies, Laurence. Only the truth. You were not responsible for Patience Merriman's death. She had a heart condition that could finish her off any moment, particularly after strenuous exertion. I can't understand you. You sound as if you positively want to be accused of killing her.'

'I did kill her,' cried Laurie. 'She was alive when I pushed that chair. I heard her cry out when it hit the wall.'

'My dear boy.' Dr Forrest was at his most authoritative. 'I really think you must be mistaken. In any case, why didn't you mention it to me before?'

'I'd forgotten. I'd got muddled.'

'You're muddled now, I think, and badly in need of rest. I'll give you a sedative.'

'No!' Laurie shook his head violently. 'I've got to stay awake in case there's news of Brenda.'

'Yes. Of course. I'm sorry. I'll go and phone now.'

Dr Forrest was not gone for long. Laurie drew back the heavy crimson curtains of the drawing-room and saw that it was already day. 'On the bald streets breaks the blank day,' he quoted to himself, and then tried hard not to think at all. It was too early to let lines from Tennyson's *In Memoriam* come into his mind: he must leave no room for anything except for hope.

'I'm afraid there's no sign of any change yet,' said Geoffrey Forrest returning to the room. 'No better but no worse either. You can go and sit in the waiting-room there if you like. I've told them you'll be coming and I'll run you round now. All right?'

'Thanks,' muttered Laurie awkwardly. He wished he could express himself more warmly, because he had every reason to feel grateful to Dr Forrest, and yet somehow he could not recapture the genuine liking and admiration that he had had for the doctor in the days when he had only known him slightly, in the days before Geoffrey Forrest's encounter with Mrs Merriman. Since then Laurie had found himself against his will seeing the doctor through Mrs Merriman's eyes, too smooth, basically selfish and self-indulgent, and somehow just not quite straight. She's poisoned my mind against him, thought Laurie, and I can't get rid of the poison.

'She was an evil woman, wasn't she,' he said suddenly when they had got into the car. 'Don't you think so?'

'Yes. Very evil,' was the curt reply.

'Don't you think she deliberately tried to kill Brenda or me or both of us?'

'Yes, I do think so,' said Geoffrey Forrest.

'Then why – '

'Then why did I spin that tale to the police?'

They turned the corner into Woodstock Road.

'I'll tell you why,' said the doctor. 'If Brenda should die – which God forbid but we can't be sure that she won't – then the police will have all the necessary information for the inquest and they will already have made up their minds how it happened. Romola will confirm that the stair-rods were loose. Suppose we try to prove that Mrs Merriman loosened them with malicious intent? We'd have to expose the whole set-up at Beechcroft. Is that what you want? For Romola to go through all that? And what about yourself? If we could by some miracle prove Patience Merriman guilty of murdering Brenda, then where does that leave you?'

'With the best possible motive for murdering Mrs Merriman myself,' cried Laurie. 'Oh, I know, I know. I've thought of it all and I suppose you're right and I suppose I ought to sound more grateful. But she ought not to have got away with it. That's what's so awful. All that viciousness being hushed up.'

'Would justice be better served,' asked Dr Forrest as they turned into the gates of the hospital, 'if you yourself were to suffer all the unpleasantness of being suspected of killing Mrs Merriman, even if no actual charge were to be made in the end?'

'Oh, I know!' cried Laurie again. 'I know I ought to thank you. And I do. It's just that – '

He could not finish the sentence. All his own deeply-held convictions about right and wrong were being turned upside down. He felt as if he had been transported from youth into the cynicism of old age within the course of a few hours.

'Anyway,' he added as they pulled up at the main door of the hospital, 'if you didn't want Mrs Merriman suspected of shifting the stair-rods, why did you plant that piece of stuff from her bed-jacket there?'

Geoffrey Forrest laughed. 'I didn't plant it. The inspector found it.'

'Well, it wasn't there before.'

'You didn't notice it, that's all.' The doctor leaned across Laurie and opened the passenger door. 'Though it's just as well for the police to think she had tried to get upstairs,' he added. 'A situation may yet arise when it would be useful to be able to show that she had loosened those rods herself. Come on. Out you get. Let's go and have a look at your young lady.'

Having a look at Brenda drove from Laurie's mind all thoughts of Mrs Merriman and Dr Forrest and every-thing and everybody else. She lay there, white and corpse-like, as if she ought to be stretched out on a mortuary slab and not on a hospital bed, except that she was surrounded by drips and tubes and cylinders and electrical equipment that gave the little room the appearance of a miniature laboratory. Laurie in his overwrought state had the nightmarish feeling that Brenda was already dead and that the whole set-up was for the purpose of con-ducting researches upon her dead body.

He stood there for a few minutes with Geoffrey Forrest gripping his arm, while white-coated figures came and went about their mysterious business. One of them had a short conversation with Dr Forrest. Laurie in his night-mare did not even hear it, but when they were walking along the corridor again the doctor said, 'She's holding her own. That's good.'

'Look.' Laurie suddenly stood still. 'If she's going to be brain-damaged – if she's just going to live like a cabbage, then for God's sake can't you just let her go?'

'There's quite a good chance,' said the doctor, still holding Laurie's arm and leading him away. 'More than fifty-fifty now, I should say. If she goes on like this another twenty-four hours the odds will be even higher. Come on. I'm taking you back to Beechcroft. There's no point in you staying here. You'll find the house feels very different now, and besides, I want you to do something for me.'

'What sort of thing?' asked Laurie listlessly.

'I want you to be some company for Romola. She likes you and she's going to be terribly shaken up by all this business. I think you will be able to help each other quite a lot.'

'I'll do my best,' said Laurie.

Dr Forrest proved right yet again. In the days that followed a close bond developed between the boy and the middle-aged woman. It was a curious companionship, born of strange circumstances, but it was completely genuine and almost completely without reserve, even when it came to discussing Romola's mother and the events that had led up to her death. The ghost of Patience Merriman lingered in the house, but the venom had gone. Beechcroft had become a different place, no longer a poisoned web of malevolence and intrigue, but just a big ugly Victorian house in which two people were doing their best to help each other through the anxious days.

Only once did the influence of Patience Merriman return with something of its former sting, and this was when the terms of her will became known. With all his other preoccupations, Laurie had temporarily forgotten about Mrs Merriman's little game with the will, but it returned vividly to his mind when Mr Edwards, looking more worried than ever, called to see Romola. They had a long conversation in the drawing-room while Laurie pottered about the garden, wondering how he could comfort Romola in what he was sure was going to be a terrible shock to her, and wishing that he himself knew more of the law so that he could talk to her more knowledgeably and helpfully.

The shock, when it came, was even worse than Laurie had expected and turned out to be a great shock for him too. Mr Edwards departed at last but Romola did not, as Laurie had expected, immediately call him in to see her. The door of the big room remained closed: the whole house took on a tense and menacing atmosphere again. After a few minutes of great anxiety Laurie decided to take the plunge and he put his head round the door. Romola did not immediately see him. She was sitting in her usual armchair with her hands lying quietly in her lap, staring out of the window. Laurie came closer but still she gave no sign that she was aware of his presence. In the end he knelt down beside her and said: 'Can I help? Or would you rather be left alone?'

She did turn round then and tried to smile.

'Oh Laurie,' she said in a strained voice. 'I ought to have called you. Geoff phoned while Mr Edwards was here to say that the specialist had just been having another look at Brenda and is very pleased with her indeed. It will take a long time, but they've no doubt at all that she will fully recover. Isn't that wonderful news?'

It was indeed wonderful news. Laurie should have been doing one of his war-dances of delight around the room, his heart singing like Maytime. It was incredible that the news that Brenda was out of danger could be so overshadowed that it did not make its full impact of joy, but that was what had happened now. The unbearable tragedy of the human life beside him gave to Laurie's glowing future the insubstantiality of a dream.

'It's wonderful,' he said, 'but what's happened, Romola? What did Mr Edwards say?'

'He came about Mother's will,' said Romola, and then stopped.

'Yes?'

Laurie looked at her with his own face beginning to twist into grief, but she avoided his eyes.

'Mother has left me nothing but the house and contents,' said Romola, biting her lip.

'Oh God!' Laurie had known it was coming but all the same he felt his eyes sting and his stomach contract in an agony of sympathy. 'Can't you contest the will?' he said.

'It's not just that.' Romola spoke as if every word brought pain. 'I can sell the house and live on the proceeds. People live on much less. It's not just the money. It's the . . . it's the . . .'

She bit her lip again and turned away, unable to say any more. Laurie did not speak, but he mentally finished the sentence for her: It's the ingratitude; it's the cruelty; it's the terrible, terrible waste of a life.

'I do think you ought to contest it, all the same,' he said presently. 'Didn't Mr Edwards suggest that you should?'

'Yes.' Romola turned to face him at last. Her voice was under control now, but the strain in her face was greater than ever. 'Yes, he did suggest it, but in the circumstances I would prefer not to. I suppose I'd better tell you at once, and get it over with. She left every bit of her money to Brenda.'

'Oh no!'

Laurie stood up and backed away from her, his mind in a turmoil. This was something for which he was totally unprepared. He moved over to the window and stood there looking out into the garden. After that first glance of horrified amazement he could not bear to look at Romola.

She seemed to be similarly affected. For a little while they both remained silent, avoiding each other's eyes. The comforting human companionship had gone completely; the poison was working again. It was Laurie who managed to dispel it. He was already developing this quality of breaking out of tangled human webs that was to serve him well in his later years of fame. He came back to where Romola was sitting, knelt down beside her, and laid a hand on her arm.

'Listen,' he said urgently, 'I don't think it was mainly meant to spite you. It was directed against Brenda and me. Don't you see? She didn't want Brenda and me to have any money, but she did want us to be suspected of killing her for her money. It was a very complicated plot, and some of it was bound to work in one way or another. Either we both tripped and killed ourselves, or one of us did and the other one guessed your mother had done it and got furious and killed your mother. Which is in fact exactly what I did when I gave the chair that push. Honestly, Romola, I would have killed your mother at that moment and I still think I did kill her, in spite of what Geoff says. She'd got it all worked out.'

'Yes,' said Romola slowly. 'Yes. I think you may be right.'

'And here's where Brenda's legacy comes in. It gives us both a motive, doesn't it? Rich old lady befriends young couple, tells them she's leaving them some money. Old lady found dead in unusual circumstances. Young couple suspected of killing her. Don't you see? If she didn't get us with her mantrap she'd have got us this other way. Isn't that just the sort of twisted thing your mother would have loved to plan?'

'Yes,' said Romola again. 'That's her trade mark. She

would have liked to think she was causing havoc from beyond the grave.'

'And she might have succeeded too,' cried Laurie getting more and more excited, 'if it hadn't been for Geoff. To think I was so annoyed with him for putting on that show for the police instead of sticking to the truth! I ought to grovel to him for the rest of my days. Of course he'd seen it all. That accounts for the fluff.'

'The fluff?' Romola looked puzzled.

'Didn't I tell you? I was quite sure that Geoff put a bit of the bed-jacket on the staircarpet for the police to find. I couldn't think what he was up to since he swore blind that your mother had died of heart failure and then he made damn sure that you and Mrs Ransome would say the stair-rods were loose. But he said to me later on that a situation might arise in which it might be useful to have some evidence that Mrs Merriman might have tried to kill Brenda or me, and this is it.'

'But it works against you too,' objected Romola. 'If Mother tried to kill Brenda, that gives you a motive for killing her.'

'Oh, I know,' said Laurie brightly. 'Geoff pointed that out too. But I'm not worried about it. Geoff will sort it all out if anything arises. He's terrific. Fancy thinking of all those possibilities in a moment like that!'

'He always thinks of everything,' said Romola in her most sombre and tragic voice. 'He's been a wonderful friend to me all these years. I couldn't possibly have coped without his support. I'd have murdered Mother myself years ago. And I've got to confess, Laurie, that I had rather hoped . . . but it will be different now, of course.'

'Of course there is no question of our keeping the

money,' said Laurie firmly. 'It's coming straight back to you.'

'No. I want you to have it,' said Romola equally firmly. 'When Brenda comes out of hospital she's going to need a great deal of attention for a long time to come. You're going to need money badly.'

'And so are you.'

They argued about it for some time, both equally determined and both equally full of goodwill. The poison had gone, never to return to Beechcroft again, and finally Romola exclaimed: 'You know, Laurie, I think we've both forgotten something very important. It's not even your money to argue about. It's been left to Brenda. And Brenda has a mind of her own. It's not functioning very well at the moment, I admit, but it will function properly again before very long. Shall we leave it to Geoff to choose the moment to tell Brenda that she is Mother's heir? And shall we then leave it to Brenda to decide what she is going to do?'

Romola looked across at Laurie. She was no longer a tragedy queen now but she was smiling, a smile that transformed her whole face.

'You know, Laurie,' she said, 'I think a very great deal of you and I value our friendship very much. Don't tell me you're going to turn into a male chauvinist pig and be furious because Brenda's got the last word. I thought you were supposed to be writing a thesis on the rights of women.'

Laurie began to laugh too. 'I am,' he said, 'and I think I'd better be getting on with it now.'